DECORATIVE PAINT PROJECTS

Over 60 Creative Designs for Furniture and Accessories

For Moira

SAFETY FIRST

It is important when using any solvent-based products to follow the manufacturer's directions carefully. Some solvents are toxic and should be handled with care. Ceramic paints should only be used on objects intended for decorative purposes; do not serve food from surfaces painted with such materials. Rags and newspapers charged up with solvent-based paints and glazes can combust if left lying around. Lay them out flat to dry before disposing of them safely.

AUTHOR'S ACKNOWLEDGMENTS

I would like to thank all the following people for the help they provided to me in different ways which enabled the book to come together: Moira Japp, Suzanne Evins, Gary Turner, Ken Birtch, Rona Fern, Mr and Mrs G. Burtt, John Anderson and Clair Mockler.

PUBLISHER'S ACKNOWLEDGMENTS

Quadrillion Publishing would like to thank Moira Japp, Janet Evins, Pam Juby and Deborah Jordan for helping to provide props.

5043 Decorative Paint Projects

Published in 1998 by CLB International, an imprint of Quadrillion Publishing Ltd, Godalming Business Centre, Woolsack Way, Godalming, Surrey GU7 1XW, England

Distributed in the US by Quadrillion Publishing Inc., 230 Fifth Avenue, New York, NY 10001
ISBN 1-85833-852-2
Printed and bound in Italy

CREDITS

Project Editor Suzanne Evins
Designer Alyson Kyles   *Photographer* Jeremy Thomas
Additional Design Louise Clements and Peter Crump
Production Neil Randles, Ruth Arthur and Karen Staff

DECORATIVE PAINT PROJECTS

DAVID JAPP

Over 60 Creative Designs for Furniture and Accessories

CLB

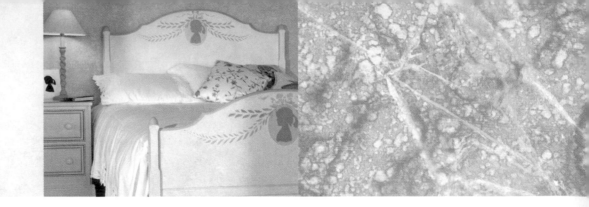

CONTENTS

Part 2
ACCESSORIES

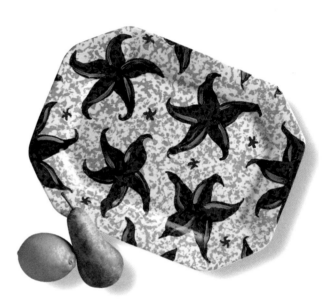

INTRODUCTION

THE AIM OF THIS BOOK is to inspire you to explore the results which can be achieved with a little imaginative use of paints and glazes. Each project and paint technique is shown in simple easy-to-follow steps and will help you gain confidence as you create unique and beautiful designs on a variety of furniture and home accessories. You do not need to be an expert to complete the projects in this book, because although some of the techniques might look daunting, approaching them in easy stages makes satisfying final results achievable—even to those with limited artistic ability.

As you browse through the book, you can choose which projects to tackle according to your level of ability. I have tried to cover and explain a broad range of paint effects on a wide number of surfaces and objects in order that you can expand your own portfolio of skills and go on to attempt more demanding techniques as your confidence grows. You do not have to follow each step religiously; you may want to use them only as a guide and add your own ideas. Don't be afraid to make mistakes; I have often found while teaching that equally satisfying results have been achieved through "happy accidents." I have also noticed that in a class of fifteen people using the exact same materials, paints, and glazes, the end results can in fact differ quite significantly. Remember that it's important to have a little of your own personality in the end result.

If you are new to paint effects, start off by attempting simpler techniques that involve easier finishes like sponging, ragging, and dragging. As you master these and learn about materials and glazes, you will feel encouraged to go on to more challenging projects like marbling and woodgraining. Versatile but simple paint techniques like stenciling and stamping are also explored as a means of creating more interest on furniture and accessories. These traditional techniques will help those of you who are less experienced to paint freehand images. By using ordinary items like sponges and potatoes imaginatively to print motifs and repeat patterns, you can easily transform the simplest of objects into something which is unique.

The philosophy behind all the projects is that they should involve minimum cost and effort. So I have deliberately chosen furniture and objects which are well past their best, in order to show how effective and versatile these paint techniques can be when trying to revitalize old and previously unwanted items. I have also included projects using cheap basic items which can be bought from mail order catalogs or home furnishings stores, to show how mass-produced everyday items can be transformed from the dull and ordinary to the extraordinary.

When I'm asked to design a themed interior, my inspiration comes from a multiplicity of sources, including natural form and the fine arts, combined with the client's own tastes. However, the most satisfaction for me comes when the finishing touches are added, vital elements that will link the interior—the furniture, wall hangings, lamps, and rugs—and pull the whole effect together. This book will hopefully inspire you to add the finishing touches to your home.

BARGAIN HUNTING

THE TWO MOST IMPORTANT things to look for when searching for furniture and accessories to work on, are condition and shape. If the object of your desire is not falling apart or riddled with woodworm and it has an appealing shape and proportions, then it is worth buying, providing that the price is right.

SOURCING JUNK

Thrift shops, junk stores, tag sales and flea markets are all worth a look, particularly for smaller items like chairs, lamps, mirrors, and picture frames. Auctions and architectural salvage yards are better for larger and more substantial items, and although these places may be a little more expensive, a purchase is worthwhile if you find an interesting piece of furniture. You should also cast a fresh eye over what you already have around the house, attic, or garage. If

you have a small piece of furniture or maybe an old lamp that is no longer useful or desirable, why not use it as a practice piece to experiment on with various techniques?

Avoid anything made from melamine or plastic. These things can only be worked on if they are well keyed to accept a coat of paint and will not be subject to excess wear and tear or heavy knocks. Look out for missing or peeling veneers on furniture, because although this can be carefully glued back or replaced, it might not be worth the effort. Solid wood items made from oak and pine are ideal, and anything made from medium-density fiberboard is particularly good for paint effects that require a smooth polished finish, for example, marbling. Be wary of hardwoods like mahogany,

because apart from the high price you will probably pay, you might end up painting on something of antique value. If you are not sure about the value or history of an object, get expert advice before you start painting it.

"DO-IT-YOURSELF" BARGAINS

If you feel a bit more adventurous and are reasonably competent with a hammer and saw, try your hand at making something simple yourself. Carpentry stores and lumber merchants will usually cut wood to given sizes, which makes it easy to produce your own hinged screen or shelving unit, which you can then customize. They also supply a wide range of moldings and decorative accessories if you want to consider adding more interest to a plain or functional item. For example, a basic chest of drawers could be given an architrave trim around the base or distinctive brass handles.

Many junk items are overlooked because of their worn or dull appearance, but as long as they are otherwise in a reasonable condition, most objects have the potential to undergo a transformation with a paint treatment.

NEW CHEAP FINDS

Perhaps the easiest objects to find and work on are new items which can be bought cheaply in home improvement centers and large department stores. The advantage of this is that items can often be bought unpainted and with no sealant on them, so with no preparation needed, you are ready to start painting instantly. Consider shelving units, chests of drawers, wardrobes, and tables, as well as lamps and picture frames. Good basic ceramics and glassware are also easiest to buy new. Fabric stores which sell end-of-roll remnants are a good place to look for canvas or other fabrics for wall hangings or floor cloths. For other soft furnishings like tablecloths and pillow covers, look in stores which sell factory seconds.

Garden and patio furniture is easily obtained in larger home improvement and garden centers and is probably best bought new if it is reasonably priced. Second-hand garden items usually have a life of their own and a certain patina about them which might be ruined with further paint treatments.

Choosing a paint effect: the same set of drawers is sanded, primed, and given two different treatments, ragged in peach and crackled in mauve and blue, to show how a finish can change the character of the same object.

TOOLS FOR THE JOB

YOU MIGHT FIND THAT you already have many of the tools and equipment needed to carry out if not most, at least some of the projects in this book. Although specialist brushes and equipment are wonderful to own and use —and usually expensive to buy—they are not always essential.

Unlike conventional painting and decorating, the tools of the specialist trade sometimes require a bit more imagination in what you use and how you apply them. All sorts of objects and materials can be used to manipulate paints and glazes—many of them ordinary household items—to create interesting marks, patterns, and textures. Old newspapers, plastic bags, feathers, sponges, toothbrushes, rags, cardboard, corks, combs, and lace— the list of armory is endless and the best way to find out what kind of effect these items can create is to practice on a prepared board. By applying a wash or glaze on to the surface and dragging, pulling, shuffling, mottling, or wiping any of these objects through it, you will see how easy it is to create interest and movement on an otherwise dull surface. This is not only fun and inspiring, it will also help you to realize the potential of your materials as a means to an end.

Below is a list and brief explanation of the tools and materials that I have used for the projects in this book. Use this list as a guide to put together your own basic toolkit.

DUSTSHEETS OR PLASTIC SHEETING

Covers are essential for protecting your carpets and furniture from dust, paint, and varnish. Recycle old sheets or blankets for this purpose and keep a supply of old newspapers on hand to cover table tops when working on smaller objects.

SCRAPERS

Hard blades of various sizes are useful for removing hard and unwanted rough patches on furniture. They are also handy for stripping heavy layers of paint and varnish when using removing agents.

FILLING OR PUTTY KNIVES

Thin flexible blades of various sizes which are used for applying hard and soft wood and two-part fillers to holes or cracks when repairing old items.

WIRE WOOL

An abrasive material which is available in a range from coarse to fine. Can be used for preparing an object by producing very fine smooth surfaces ready for painting. It is also good for rubbing back layers of paint to create a distressed look.

A basic toolkit will include a few standard decorating tools used for various jobs, some specialist items like a natural sponge, a feather, and a rocker, plus a number of household items such as rags, newspapers, and a toothbrush.

SANDPAPERS

Different textures of sandpaper are also available from coarse to fine. Use to smooth down rough surfaces and filled areas before painting, and to distress a painted surface. The finer, quality papers—cabinet paper, glass paper, and wet and dry paper—should be used to rub down the base coat for effects which require a very smooth surface, such as marble and tortoiseshell.

MASKING TAPE

Good for protecting areas from paint, masking off paneled areas and for providing an edge in order to paint straight lines. It can also be used to create shapes and curves, with a little patience. Choose the low-tack variety to avoid damaging or lifting any previously painted surfaces.

STRAIGHT EDGE

Use a ruler or improvise with a piece of molding to help steady your hand when painting lines, areas of detail or when marking out paneling. This is also a useful item to hit your brush against when spattering.

THE VERSATILE DUSTING BRUSH

These cheap dusting brushes are a perfect example of how brushes old and new can still be used for a variety of jobs and techniques, without the need to spend money on a set of purpose-made brushes. The new brush is ideal for dragging, flogging, stippling, and softening; the middle-aged brush for colorwashing and aging; and the old brush for heavy-duty distressing and working glazes into areas of detail.

CONTAINERS

Always keep a variety of lidded containers on hand for mixing and storing paint, from paint trays to household items like glass jars and ice cream containers. However, do not use plastic containers with oil-based paints, as they may melt the plastic.

BRUSHES

These can be divided into three types: conventional decorating brushes in a variety of shapes and sizes to use for preparatory work; specialist brushes for specific tasks like graining and softening; and a selection of artist's brushes for delicate line work, picking out areas of detail, and for freehand painting. Purchase specialist items only as and when you need them.

RADIATOR ROLLERS

These decorating tools are available in various textures from smooth to heavy pile. They are ideal to cover large areas of an object with paint, or if you want to add texture to a painted surface.

SPONGES

Both synthetic household sponges and natural sponges are essential for making distinctive marks and textures for many different finishes. Always use a natural sponge where indicated, as a synthetic one is no substitute.

BLOTTING MATERIALS

This includes items like rags, newspapers, plastic wrap, tissue paper, and plastic bags, which can be used for making marks for a wide variety of finishes when applied to wet paints or glazes.

FEATHERS

A range of sizes is essential for creating veins in marbling. Find them on the shore or in woodland, otherwise you can buy them in artist's suppliers.

GRAINING TOOLS

These include household combs and pieces of cardboard for creating woodgrained effects and other interesting marks. A heartgrainer or "rocker" can be bought from good home improvement centers or artist's suppliers to produce authentic-looking woodgrains.

STAMPING TOOLS

These can be created from a wide variety of things from potatoes, carrots, or rutabagas, to sponges and pieces of rubber. Cut vegetable stamps should be wiped on paper towel first to remove any starch before applying any paint.

CRAFT KNIFE & SCISSORS

A good craft knife is essential for cutting sharp stencils, templates, and decoupage images. A cutting mat is a worthwhile investment, otherwise cut out on a thick piece of cardboard. A small pair of household scissors is also useful to have for simpler cutting jobs.

ONE TOOL, MANY JOBS

It is not necessary to buy a lot of specialist equipment to ensure the best results. Versatile tools such as a good dusting brush or wallpaper brush can be used for a variety of projects. Not only for applying the glaze in the first place, but also when stippling, dragging, flogging, colorwashing, graining, distressing, and even gently softening.

STENCILING MATERIAL

Apart from purpose-made stencil card, other materials which can be used to cut stencils are acetate, a thin clear film available in rolls, or plastic portfolio sleeves, which are cheap and durable.

SPRAY ADHESIVE

Use repositional spray adhesive for holding stencils, so they can be removed without leaving behind a residue or damaging the surface. Permanent spray adhesive should be used for decoupage images.

The best tools are those which can be used time and again. The paint on this acetate stencil testifies to the fact that it has provided good service on a number of projects.

SURFACE PREPARATION

THE ENORMOUS ARRAY OF different surfaces on which to paint can be confusing and irritating to the keen decorator who wants to get started. In order to achieve successful and satisfying end results, however, it is essential to invest some time and effort at the initial stages of preparation to avoid later disappointments.

Most decorative paint treatments require sound preparation, especially those highly polished and sophisticated effects like marbling, tortoiseshelling, and some imitation hardwoods and inlays. Even more straightforward finishes like dragging, ragging, and stippling require a reasonably smooth surface. Sponging and colorwashing are probably the only two treatments that can be applied successfully to almost any surface, whatever the level of previous preparation. In contrast, effects which try to create the appearance of aging and distressing are not only helped by less refined surfaces, but are enhanced by them because of their inherent texture and flaws. When attempting to make an object or piece of furniture look older than it really is, don't fill the knocks and dents, but use them to your advantage by highlighting them with rubbed-in antiquing glazes.

When dealing with such a wide variety of surfaces, it is important to use the appropriate preparation techniques and relevant primers. The following list gives general advice on how to prepare and prime the various surfaces you will encounter in this book.

NEW WOOD

If you want to have a completely painted finish (rather than see the woodgrain), it is best to prime and seal the surface with an acrylic primer. If you want some of the wood to show through, seal it first with shellac sanding sealer or thinned-down varnish. It will then need to be smoothed over with fine sandpaper.

OLD WOOD

Previously painted or varnished pieces have to be "keyed" to accept new paint. If you have to remove the layers of paint completely, buy a paint or varnish stripper and follow the directions carefully. If the item is in reasonable condition, however, this might not be necessary. A good rub down with medium, then fine sandpaper should make the surface smooth enough, then wipe it over with a rag and some mineral spirits and apply two coats of oil-based paint as a base coat.

METAL

New metal should be cleaned first with detergent and water. Older or second-hand metal should be rubbed over and any rust removed with steel wool and mineral spirits, or coarse sandpaper. Then prepare the surface by applying a coat of red oxide metal primer or universal primer and two coats of oil-based paint as a base coat. Spray paints can also be used as a base coat, as they adhere well to most surfaces.

FABRIC

Apart from a thorough wash, fabric generally doesn't need any preparation as long as good quality fabric paints are used and you follow the manufacturer's directions.

CERAMICS

It can be difficult to get paints to adhere to ceramic objects because of their durable polished surfaces. Abrasive materials which are usually used for keying will only scratch, rather than smooth, the surface. Therefore, it is usually sufficient simply to wash ceramic items with detergent and water, or to apply a very light abrasive.

GLASS

All items should be handled with care. The surface should be washed with detergent and water or neat vinegar and dried before any paint is applied.

CARDBOARD

An acrylic primer should be applied to any cardboard, then smoothed over with fine sandpaper before continuing with the relevant base coat.

PLASTER

Untreated plaster is a very absorbent material and it is impossible to apply any paint to the surface before it is sealed. Do this with either shellac or thinned acrylic primer. Alternatively, use a solution of wood glue with an equal amount of water, applying to the surface quickly.

TERRA-COTTA & STONE

These natural materials are both very absorbent and should usually be sealed with a thinned-down universal primer or shellac. However, for the projects in this book I have used this characteristic absorbency to help create the effect I wanted and thinned the paints and glazes so that they disappeared into the material.

Paints & Glazes

An almost infinite amount of interest, depth, and movement can be created on furniture and accessories by the clever use of paints and glazes. This is now made much easier for the less experienced by the increasing availability of substances that, until recently, could only be found in specialist trade suppliers. It is no surprise that paint and glaze manufacturers have now realized the market potential of unconventional paint techniques. You no longer have to hunt for what once were obscure products like crackle varnish or acrylic scumble, you can now buy them in most home improvement centers. This gives you an almost bewildering range of finishes to choose from and with that a confusing choice of media in which to work.

Unless working on a specific material that requires its own specially manufactured products, like fabric or ceramic paints, most of the paint techniques in this book are applied in either water- or oil-based paints or glazes. Both mediums have their advantages that might make them more suitable for one particular technique. For example, marbling looks more convincing when painted in oils, so it pays to prepare the object using oil-based primers and base coat and protect the finish with oil-based varnish. On the other hand, a peeled and cracked paint technique is more successful using water-based paints. A good general rule is to stick with either oil- or water-based products throughout a project.

Oil-based glazes and colors take longer to dry; each coat should be left overnight before another layer is applied. However, this can be an advantage, allowing more time to make patterns on the surface and manipulate the glaze. This is especially helpful for the beginner when trying more difficult techniques like marbling and woodgraining.

Water-based paints and glazes have the benefit of being more user-friendly and safer to use because they produce less hazardous fumes, and materials like brushes and sponges are much easier to clean by soaking in water. They also dry faster and this has the advantage of letting you apply more than one layer in a day, which is useful for colorwashing or for aging and distressing an object.

Apart from the occasional use of more unusual products that are not water- or oil-based such as sprays or metallic paints, most of the paints and glazes used throughout the book are fairly standard and can be obtained quite easily in home improvement centers.

Primers

Quick-drying acrylic primer can be used to prepare and seal new wood. Universal primer can be used for a variety of materials, including wood and metal. For metals, a red oxide primer can also be used, available as a spray.

Latex Paint

A standard water-based paint which can be bought in an almost infinite choice of colors and thinned to produce a semitransparent glaze. Can be tinted with universal stainers or artist's acrylic colors. Available in a mat or silk finish.

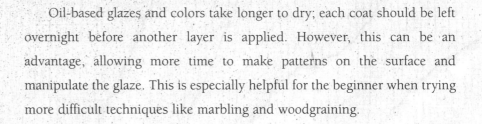

GLASS PAINTS
The three primary colors—red, yellow and blue —can be mixed to create a varied palette.

WAX CRAYONS
Use on fabric to create a resist and to provide a sharp clear line instead of using a brush.

APPLYING PAINT

Use a brush, roller, or spray to apply paint, mixing your own colors, where possible, to create the right shade.

OIL-BASED PAINTS

Available in a number of finishes including undercoat, semigloss, satin, or gloss. Can be thinned with mineral spirits and tinted with artist's oil colors. Oil-based paints are slow-drying and durable, but must be used in a well-ventilated area because of the fumes and handled with care.

ACRYLIC COLORS

Artist's water-based paints which are ideal for any watercolor work and for tinting water-based paints and glazes.

ARTIST'S OIL COLORS

As their name suggests, these are oil-based colors, which can be used suspended in mineral spirits to tint oil-based paints and glazes, as well as polyurethane varnishes.

ACRYLIC SCUMBLE GLAZE

A slow-drying, water-based glaze which can be thinned with water and tinted with artist's acrylic colors or water-based paints, then used for a variety of paint techniques. It produces little or no fumes and won't yellow with age. It dries to a more mat finish than oil-based scumble.

OIL-BASED SCUMBLE GLAZE

A glaze which can be tinted with oil-based paints or artist's oil colors. It is transparent and when applied can be manipulated with ease because it is slow-drying.

CRACKLE VARNISH

A two-part commercial varnish used together to create fine, delicate cracks to give the appearance of age.

CRACKLE MEDIUM

A water-based product which is applied between two layers of water-based paints in contrasting colors. This causes the top layer to crack and peel, depending on the thickness of the applications.

SPRAY PAINT

Available in artist's suppliers or more cheaply as automobile sprays. Must be used in a well-ventilated area, wearing a mask.

METALLIC PAINTS

These come in a variety of colors, but gold, silver, and bronze are most useful for highlighting details.

SPECIALIST PAINTS

Paints for fabrics and ceramics are designed to work with these materials. Fabric paints are designed not to spread or bleed, and are washable. Ceramic paints are available as solvent and water-based products. Follow the manufacturer's directions, as they are not always suitable for surfaces which will be used for food and drink.

TINTED WAX

Gold, silver, and bronze waxes are available in artist's suppliers and are ideal for applying small finishing touches.

INCANDESCENT PAINT
A water-based paint with a unique pearlescent finish.

SPECIALIST PAINTS
A range of specialist fabric, glass, ceramic, and metallic paints are available from artist's suppliers or craft stores for use on specific surfaces.

FINISHING & PROTECTING

DO NOT UNDERESTIMATE THE importance of adding a finishing layer of varnish or wax to your painted object. Whether for protection or to enhance the appearance, it is essential that it is applied with care and patience or it will detract and possibly ruin all the hard work you have done up to this point.

As a general rule, you should keep your medium constant, so that if you have used water-based primer and paint on your object, you should protect it with water-based varnish. As much as possible, try to varnish in a dust-free environment, keeping windows closed. Try to look at the object against a good light; this way you will see any obvious brushmarks or mistakes and will be able to rectify them while the varnish is still wet. A good tip if you need durability is to apply up to three or four coats of high gloss varnish and then two coats of your required finish on top, for example, satin or mat.

ACRYLIC VARNISH

Acrylic or water-based varnishes are the easiest to use. Although they appear milky in the container, they dry to a clear, completely transparent, protective film, are very easy to apply, and dry quickly allowing for many coats, if necessary, in one day. Some acrylic varnishes are extremely durable and can be used to protect floors and other areas subject to heavy wear and tear, but these are not always widely available.

A tint can be added to the varnish using water-based paints or artist's acrylic colors. However, it can be difficult to judge how much color to add and you might rely on trial and error until you get used to compensating for the milky appearance of the wet varnish.

WET ACRYLIC VARNISH
When it is first applied straight from the tin, the varnish has an opaque milky appearance.

DRY ACRYLIC VARNISH
As it dries, the cloudiness disappears to a barely noticeable clear, transparent film.

TINTED ACRYLIC VARNISH
Alternatively, it can be tinted with other water-based paints to add extra color or an aging effect to a painted surface.

TWO-PART VARNISHES
These varnishes have the most durable finish, but are unpleasant and difficult to use, so are not recommended for the inexperienced.

POLYURETHANE VARNISH

Tint with artist's oil colors to create a range of natural-looking finishes, or color with white oil-based paint to produce a wash effect.

POLYURETHANE VARNISH

Oil-based or polyurethane varnishes are widely available and have the advantage of being very durable when dry and resistant to most stains and heavy knocks. However, they are much harder to apply properly and require overnight drying between coats. Another disadvantage is their tendency to yellow with age and especially in rooms starved of light. When using solvent-based varnishes it is better to build up thin, even layers rather than try to apply it straight from the can, thickly, in one coat. Thin the varnish with about 20% mineral spirits and apply three or four even layers, avoiding runs and thick or thin patches.

An advantage of oil and polyurethane varnishes is that they are easier to tint, using artist's oil colors or semigloss paint, in order to alter the finished color of the object.

As these varnishes need overnight drying, this can result in dust and grit settling on the object. So it is important to rub over the surface gently with wet and dry sandpaper or fine cabinet paper dipped in warm water, between each additional coat.

OTHER VARNISHES

Various two-part mixtures made from oil and water are available. They are extremely durable and hardwearing, but should be avoided because they are unpleasant to use and hazardous if you do not follow the manufacturer's directions carefully. Also, because of their very fast drying times, it is essential that you work very quickly.

TINTED BEESWAX

A wax finish may be more appropriate for a decorative wood or marbled treatment, and they are available with various wood-finish tints, like antique pine. While a wax finish imparts a lovely natural luster to an object, it will not protect the surface from hard knocks or hot objects.

TINTED & UNTINTED BEESWAX

Always use natural beeswax to add a traditional polished patina to a surface – the more layers the better. A tinted wax will add extra warmth and color.

HOW TO USE COLOR

MODERN MANUFACTURERS OFFER AN almost endless range of colored paints and glazes, and the end result achieved using them can be more than satisfactory. However, buying these ready-made colors cannot compare with the pleasure and resulting quality of mixing your own.

CREATING TRADITIONAL COLORS

It is worth remembering at this stage that most colors come from powdered pigments. Historically, these pigments would have come from the earth in the form of ground rocks, minerals, or vegetable matter, and suspended in a binder, like linseed oil or egg yolk, then thinned with turpentine or water. Many of today's pigments and paints are synthetically produced and although much more convenient and cheaper to use, there is often a lack of quality and sophistication about them. It is for this reason that more and more companies are trying to recreate that "feel of the past" by using natural ingredients to mix more "historical" colors.

If you want to improve your color-mixing talents and have fun experimenting, start with a basic palette of three primary colors, for example, cadmium red, cadmium yellow, and French ultramarine blue, in artist's oil colors (if you want to work in a water-based medium, substitute acrylic colors for artist's oils and use with water-based latex paint instead of oil-based semigloss). In order to transform these "pure" primaries into viable decorating colors (assuming that you do not want to use them unadulterated), you will need to add one or a combination of the natural earth colors: raw umber, burnt umber, raw sienna, burnt sienna, and yellow ocher. You might also need black, but remember that the more black you add to a color, the more lifeless it becomes. For this reason the earth colors are so important because they can be used to warm or cool, lighten, or darken a color without it losing its quality.

YELLOW OCHER

RAW SIENNA

Try squeezing a little of each primary onto a nonabsorbent surface and see what happens when you add a little white and a bit of one of the earth colors, or vice versa. As you become more confident you might find that you have to add more colors to your palette to extend your range, particularly darker hues like Prussian blue or viridian green. You might also like to try mixing the earth colors together with a

COLOR WHEEL
Harmonious color schemes derive from colors close to each other on the wheel, while contrasting schemes come from colors opposite each other.

BLUE

VIOLET

YELLOW

RED

GREEN

ORANGE

PRIMARY AND SECONDARY COLORS
The primary colors are red, blue and yellow. The secondary colours, violet, green and orange, are created by mixing two primaries.

EARTH COLORS

The five earth colors are essential to creating quality, traditional colors. They can be either mixed with the primary colors, or blended together with the addition of black or white to lighten or darken.

BURNT SIENNA

BURNT UMBER

RAW UMBER

HARMONIOUS COLORS

A simple exercise is to see how you can improve the quality and "feel" of standard paint color (in this case orange, center) by adding a small amount of its complementary color (in this case blue), the earth colors, and white. This will give you a range of colors from earthy terra-cotta to a dusky salmon pink. (In a clockwise direction the dish shows the addition of: blue (left), burnt umber, yellow ocher, white, burnt sienna, and raw umber.)

little white, for example, yellow ocher and raw umber, mixed with a little white can result in an elegant creamy parchment color.

CHOOSING COLOR SCHEMES

Whether you are looking to rework a whole interior, or simply choosing colors for a new project to fit into an existing scheme, it is important to remember that everyone's visual response to color is highly personal. The use of color's emotive qualities can be manipulated by its surroundings, and for this reason, you should never see or judge color in isolation.

There are three basic color schemes from which you can develop the mood of your interior: monochromatic, harmonious, and contrasting. When choosing a color scheme, think in terms of color combinations and the final result that you want to achieve. For example, a monochromatic scheme using a variety of shades of the same color, would create a warm atmosphere if golden yellows or Venetian reds are used, but alternatively would create a cool interior if used with blue-grays or greens. Also consider that in general terms warm colors are considered "advancing" which will make a room look smaller, whereas cool colors appear to "retreat" resulting in a more spacious feel.

Developing a harmonious scheme requires a little more thought, but is easier on the eye because it blends different colors which are close to each other on the color wheel but similar in tone or shade. Contrasting color schemes are for the more adventurous. They are harder to create

successfully and need a more courageous approach because they work on the principle that colors at the opposite ends of the color spectrum complement each other, although if used cleverly they can be lively and rewarding.

If you find it difficult to initiate a color scheme, why not look at a favorite object or something which you might have in your home? Inspiration can come from anywhere, an old plate, pillow, or rug, for example, and think about why you like these things, is it the color, the color combinations, or varying proportions of color? It is always worth the time to plan and experiment with colors before embarking on a new scheme, avoiding costly mistakes at a later stage.

COLOR SCHEMES

A monochromatic scheme using a variety of shades of the same color.

PART 1
FURNITURE

COLORWASHED PEG RACK

CHECKLIST

*green and white water-based
    paints*

medium-size brushes

fine artist's brush

rag

potato

craft knife

pale blue water-based paint

acrylic varnish

THIS TECHNIQUE OF APPLYING thin washes of color on to untreated wood, is a finish reminiscent of liming. Traditionally, open-grain woods like oak were treated with a lime paste to protect them from insect infestation, but the method became popular as a decorative wood treatment in the seventeenth century when people realized that in certain circumstances the milky paste enhanced the characteristics and appearance of the wood.

In recent years, artists and craftsmen have explored various methods of application using thinned plaster, thinned oil- and water-based paints, and an assorted mixture of tinted waxes. For this treatment on a piece of untreated pine board (originally a pine shelf cut to shape), I chose a green water-based paint and thinned it to a consistency of light cream. It is important to get this mixture right and it depends on the quality (thickness) of the paint that you use, so it is wise to experiment first on an offcut of board. The aim is to create a transluscent effect using this colored wash, rather than opaque paint, letting the grain and any other characteristics of the wood show through. As well as creating more depth and interest, it is also a quick and easy way to co-ordinate and revitalize existing or new wooden items into your colour scheme.

*The simplicity of this Shaker-style coat rack lies in the fact
that it can be created from a recycled pine shelf and wooden
dowels, and colorwashed with a few subtle colors to
enhance, rather than mask, the beauty of the wood.*

STEP 1
Thin a green water-based paint with about 70% water and brush it over the whole object.

STEP 2
While the paint is still wet, rub the excess off with a clean rag; this will help push the color into the grain. Leave to dry for a few hours.

STEP 3
Repeat the process but using a thinned off-white water-based paint instead. Again leave to dry for a few hours.

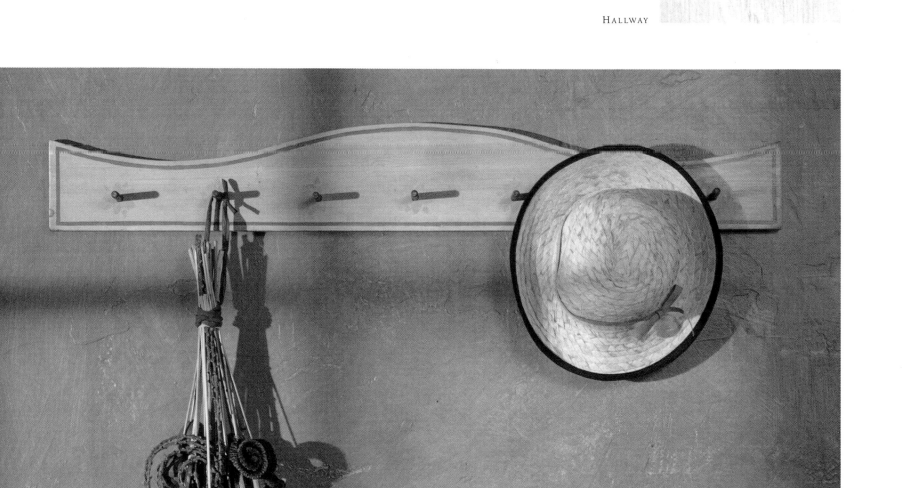

STEP 4
Mix a darker green color and using a small artist's brush, paint a fine line around the edges to accentuate the shape.

STEP 5
Slice a potato in half and carefully cut a flower shape into it; use this to stamp a motif in pale blue in the position where the pegs will be attached. Leave to dry and protect with a coat of acrylic varnish.

FLOATING MARBLE & GILDED CONSOLE TABLE

CHECKLIST

red oxide primer spray paint

gold spray paint

medium-size brushes

white oil-based semigloss

masking tape

amber and brown French enamel varnish

methylated spirits

French ultramarine blue and black artist's oil colors

oil-based scumble glaze

mineral spirits

toothbrush

rag

acetate and craft knife

spray adhesive

gold oil-based paint

feather

gloss polyurethane varnish

THIS TABLE WAS AN EXCELLENT find at an auction because although it was covered in layers of heavy brown gloss paint, it was in very good condition and needed only a flick over with medium, then fine sandpaper to provide a key on which to paint.

Since console tables traditionally have a gilded base and a solid marble top, I did not have to think twice about a suitable paint finish. The combination of marbling on the top and shelf, and patinated gilding on the legs, adds an elegant classical touch which helps to give the table an effect of weight and substance. These techniques combined can work very well on a variety of items and although the finished result looks difficult to achieve, it is more a question of technique and materials than artistic ability.

French enamel varnish which is used for the effect on the legs, is a ready-dyed shellac (like the sealer used for knotting bare wood before it is painted), which has many advantages that make it worthwhile searching out. Apart from the pure and beautiful translucent colors it

produces, it dries very quickly and to a strong durable finish which has a seductive shine to it. It can be thinned with methylated spirits if you want to reduce the shine and have a slightly longer working time. If you cannot obtain French enamel varnish, replace this with oil-based scumble glaze colored with artist's oil colors in burnt sienna and burnt umber, and use mineral spirits as a dispersant instead of methylated spirits.

As a base coat to work on, I sprayed the legs and sides of the table with red oxide metal primer and prepared the top and lower shelf with two coats of white oil-based semigloss paint. When applying the varnish, ensure that you tilt the table as you work, so that you are always working on a horizontal surface to avoid runs.

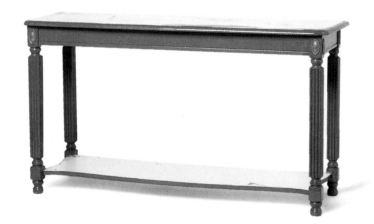

STEP 1

Mask off the areas you don't want painted. Spray the sides and legs of the table with gold spray and leave to dry.

STEP 2

Working quickly, brush on patches of amber-colored French enamel varnish thinned with a little methylated spirits.

STEP 3

Immediately brush on more patches of darker-brown French enamel varnish.

STEP 4

Flick splashes of methylated spirits lightly over the surface to disperse the varnishes and leave to dry.

STEP 5

Mix a deep-blue glaze using French ultramarine blue and a little black artist's oil color, 50% oil-, and 50% mineral spirits. Apply it to the top and shelf of the table.

STEP 6

While this glaze is still wet, dab it lightly with a clean rag to even it all over the surface, creating a soft mottled effect.

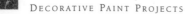

STEP 7

While the glaze is still wet, flick on droplets of mineral spirits and some gold oil-based paint thinned with a little mineral spirits, to disperse the glaze and leave to dry completely.

STEP 8

Using the Greek key template, stencil the image in gold using the flower to mark the center of the shelf and top.

STEP 9

Leave the stencil to dry, then reverse it and using the flower as your registration mark, stencil the other half.

STEP 10

Let the whole table dry overnight, then varnish with at least two coats of gloss polyurethane varnish. As an additional step, you may wish to apply some veining using a feather and a white oil-based paint.

The patinated gold effect on the legs and base and marbling on the top and bottom shelves, makes this console table a dramatic and classical focal point for any hallway.

CLASSICAL GILDED MIRROR

CHECKLIST

brown-red water-based paint

medium-size brushes

tissue paper

gold wax

rag

kitchen scourer

black water-based paint

gloss polyurethane varnish

THE ART OF REAL GILDING takes an enormous amount of patience and skill, which takes many years to master and perfect. This is why gilding is such a costly exercise. Traditionally, this would involve painstakingly sanding the object, which could be made in wood or cast in plaster, applying up to ten layers of gesso (a mixture of glue and whiting), then delicately covering the surface in wafer-thin sheets of gold before burnishing.

Although there are a number of less time-consuming ways to embellish an object in a gilded fashion, this particular technique is simple and effective. It can transform almost any decorative object with stunning results and without the expense of many gilding methods, which makes it a versatile finish, particularly for mirror and picture frames as well as smaller items such as jewelry boxes and lamp bases. This large mirror would have been prohibitively expensive to gild using any other method.

Gilding is also a convincing way to add authenticity and an antique feel to an object, conjuring up almost instant results which rely more on simple technique than hard work or creative skill.

STEP 1

Paint the whole mirror frame in a brown-red water-based paint. While this is still wet, loosely cover the surface in tissue paper ensuring that you keep some of the wrinkles.

STEP 2

Before the paint under the tissue paper dries, paint over the surface again in the brown-red mixture and leave to dry.

STEP 3

Apply a gold wax over the surface of the object, rubbing in with a soft rag.

STEP 4

After a few minutes, burnish the surface with a kitchen scourer, rubbing particularly hard on raised areas to reveal some of the underlying red color.

STEP 5

Flick small dots of thinned black paint here and there with a toothbrush for added interest. Leave to dry and if necessary varnish with a coat of gloss polyurethane varnish.

The imitation gilding on this mirror frame helps to lend a classical and elegant touch to this hallway, creating the effect of light and space in an often dark area of the home.

LIVING ROOM

LAPIS LAZULI COFFEE TABLE

CHECKLIST

*white oil-based semigloss
    paint*

medium-size brushes

mineral spirits

oil-based scumble glaze

*French ultramarine blue
    artist's oil color*

black artist's oil color

masking tape

acetate and craft knife

spray adhesive

gold paint and wax

rag

WHEN I DISCOVERED THIS table, it was a cheap and rather basic item in a second-hand shop, but it was easily transformed into a more robust-looking coffee table with a few architectural moldings bought at the local hardware store. I then had to decide on a suitable paint treatment that would intensify the appearance of weight and solidity.

Lapis lazuli is a deep-blue mineral which, because of its traditional use as a source of ultramarine pigment, became quite scarce, and hence became sought in its polished form as a gemstone and for use in decorative inlay. Before you begin, try to get hold of either a small piece of lapis or a photograph to work from. This will help you observe the marks and density of color you are trying to achieve and also serve as inspiration. The aim is not to copy the real thing, but to try to emulate the overall appearance.

To imitate lapis lazuli successfully, it is important to work on a smooth surface. Prepare the object by smoothing over with medium-grade then fine sandpaper. Wipe over with a damp rag and when dry, apply an even layer of white oil-based undercoat. Let this dry overnight and then sand over gently with fine cabinet paper to remove any bits of dust which might have settled overnight. Then apply another layer of white oil-based undercoat and let this dry completely, again overnight.

STEP 1
Mix a thin glaze from 60% mineral spirits and 40% oil-based scumble glaze and add French ultramarine blue artist's oil color. Apply and stipple this glaze over the entire surface.

STEP 2
While the glaze is wet, dip a clean brush into mineral spirits and spatter randomly onto the glaze by hitting the brush against a piece of wood over the surface. This will disperse the glaze unevenly.

STEP 3
Again, while the glaze is still wet, mix some oil-based gold paint with a little mineral spirits and spatter in random patches with a toothbrush. Leave to dry completely.

STEP 4

Mask off a border about 2 inches inside the edge of the table and apply more of the original blue glaze but with a little black artist's oil color added to the mixture, to make it slightly darker. Leave to dry.

STEP 5

Mask off a thin border around the edge and rub in a line of gold wax, using a rag. Continue by stenciling classical patterns using gold paint. Protect and enhance the finish with satin polyurethane varnish.

The addition of a few moldings, strong lapis lazuli colors, and a bold stencil in gold, gives what was once a cheap and unstable melamine table real weight and substance.

Pewter-effect Fireplace

This Edwardian cast-iron fireplace was found rusting and abandoned in a local architectural salvage yard. It was covered in many layers of paint and varnish (about 12 on close inspection!) from its previous owners and it would have been a messy and time-consuming process to strip them all off.

Instead, I decided to try to imitate the effect that would have resulted if it had been professionally sandblasted back to its original state. Using basic materials and equipment, this simple and effective treatment can be used to add visual weight and interest to almost any object.

This method is particularly useful if you already have an old fireplace installed in your home, as you can work on the fireplace *in situ*. This gets around the inconvenience of either removing it or stripping off any layers of paint.

It is important to note that if you decide to apply this technique to a fire surround that incorporates a real fire, you will need to use specialist paints. You should substitute a specialist metallic-silver paint suitable to withstand high temperatures for the base coat and use fire-black or an equivalent paint (normally used to paint fire grilles) for the top distressing coat.

STEP 1

Prepare the surface first by brushing on a metallic-silver paint and leaving to dry. Then apply a full coat of black water-based paint thinned slightly with water.

STEP 2

Working quickly and using a dry brush, work this paint into the moldings and at the same time remove the excess paint, revealing the silver color underneath. As you do this, keep wiping the brush clean on a rag.

STEP 3

After you have removed most of the black paint, leave it to dry completely. Rub over with fine wire wool to bring up more of the metallic-silver color, if this is necessary.

STEP 4

Tap the top of a silver spray paint can with a piece of wood in order to spatter small areas of silver to sharpen the effect.

This is a quick and relatively simple technique to restore an old fireplace. There is no preparation needed, as it can be applied straight on to many layers of paint.

ORIENTAL CALLIGRAPHY SCREEN

CHECKLIST

black spray paint

red oil-based paint

mineral spirits

medium-size brushes

gold oil-based paint

toothbrush

black oil-based paint

medium-weight cotton canvas

size 8 artist's brush

size 3 artist's brush

THIS OLD VANITY SCREEN was a lucky find in a junk store. I had been looking out for something that might work with an Eastern theme for some time and snapped this up the moment I saw it, as the delicate framework and detailed spindles are perfect for what I had in mind.

Before embarking on the project, I smoothed the metal frame over quickly with fine wire wool. Spray paint is ideal for this sort of object as it is much quicker than trying to paint all the fiddly details with a small brush, and also has the advantage of drying very quickly Do remember always to work in a well-covered and ventilated area when using spray paints.

For the fabric panels I used a medium-weight cotton duck canvas, especially as the natural yellowy color was reminiscent of parchment. The abstract shapes painted on the fabric were inspired by Chinese characters, but if you don't feel confident enough to paint them on freehand, then pencil the images lightly on to the fabric first. When fully dry, the fabric can be ironed carefully using a low heat and attached to the screen using glue.

If you cannot get hold of an appropriately shaped screen, why not improvise by making your own with thick dowels and wood glue? Most lumber merchants will cut wood to given sizes for a small fee.

STEP 1
Spray the screen with a gloss black paint. When dry, spatter with a red oil-based paint (thinned with a little mineral spirits) by hitting a loaded brush against a piece of wood.

STEP 2
Flick smaller dots of gold oil-based paint randomly over the surface, using a toothbrush.

STEP 3
Cut three pieces of canvas to the appropriate size and paint broad calligraphic shapes in black paint (thinned with a little mineral spirits) with a size 8 artist's brush.

STEP 4

Paint the smaller red shapes as a contrast in thinned red paint with a size 3 artist's brush.

STEP 5

To add a contrast to the sharp calligraphy, splash randomly over selected areas with more of the thinned black paint.

This is a good example of how a simple technique with bold colors and shapes can be used to create a distinctive piece of furniture. Creating successful oriental lettering relies on a little practice and using good quality artist's brushes.

STENCILED OCCASIONAL TABLE

CHECKLIST

*white and gray oil-based
    semigloss paint*

medium-size brushes

mineral spirits

oil-based scumble glaze

rag

*light blue, pink, green, and
    off-white water-based paint*

natural sponge

acetate and craft knife

spray adhesive

fine artist's brush

satin polyurethane varnish

THIS OLD ROUND-TOPPED table was bought for next to nothing because it looked so tired and worn. I liked its neat shape and thought it would be ideal when fixed up for use as a delicate and unobtrusive occasional table. The term "occasional" was originally used for small tables which weren't in regular use, but small pieces of furniture like this have now come into their own and are ideal for displaying flowers and favorite photographs.

After a few minor repairs to the legs and a bit of glue here and there, I sanded the previously painted surface (many layers) with medium- then fine-grade paper in order to provide a key for two layers of white oil-based semigloss as a base coat.

For the stenciled image, I wanted a simple motif which would echo the shape of the table top, so I copied and simplified an old holly wreath drawing. The three-dimensional effect was created by two-stage stippling, stenciling the first coat in three different colors, leaving to dry, then repositioning it on the same spot to create a "shadow" to be stippled in white.

When the whole table was dry, I picked out some of the details and moldings using a fine artist's brush dipped in one of the stenciled colors thinned with a little water (add a drop of liquid detergent to this to help it flow better). The finished result should be varnished to protect the surface.

STEP 1
Mix a glaze with 50% mineral spirits and 50% oil-based scumble and add a tiny amount of gray oil-based paint. Apply over the entire surface and gently dab with a soft rag to create a subtle, mottled effect. Leave to dry.

STEP 2
Continue to add depth to the table top by sponging a light-green water-based paint evenly over the surface. Leave to dry.

STEP 3
Position the stencil in the middle of the table and stipple a light blue and a pink water-based paint in patches. Leave to dry.

STEP 4

Remove the stencil carefully and reposition back on top of the image, moving it slightly so that it does not register exactly.

STEP 5

Stipple an off-white water-based paint gently through the template and remove the stencil. Embellish the table further with the leaf stencil around the sides in the same colors and with the cyclamen stencil in the center stippled in green and deep pink. Finally, protect with a coat of varnish.

Though an occasional table like this is a functional item, it can also be transformed into a highly decorative piece of furniture with sponging and stencils—so you may not want to hide it with lamps or pictures.

FLEUR-DE-LIS WALL HANGING

CHECKLIST

medium-weight cotton canvas

tracing paper

pencil

fine artist's brush

medium-size brush

liquid frisket

gold oil-based paint

blue and violet spray paints

THIS IS THE IDEAL project if you want to create your own highly stylized and individual work of art, but lack confidence when it comes to being creative with paint. Although I have used fairly common images like freehand squiggles and fleur-de-lis motifs, you can source your own images from almost anywhere—look for inspiration from magazines, wallpaper, or printed fabric—and transfer the shapes on to the fabric by copying them on to tracing paper.

This particular project evolved from some experimental techniques I was using on fabric. By trying to achieve an interesting three-dimensional quality on a flat piece of fabric, I arrived at a look that combines a medieval and contemporary feel. I used medium-weight cotton duck canvas, but you can experiment and achieve different effects by using lighter- or heavier-weight fabrics such as muslin, sailcloth, or fine silk. If you can't get hold of artist's liquid frisket (usually available at good art suppliers), replace this with wood glue thinned slightly with water. Either method will help to produce the slightly three-dimensional look reminiscent of the effects created by using batik techniques.

When the project was finished, I glued under the raw edges on the left and right sides, and cut out a tab top at both ends of the wall hanging. The edges were glued over a decorative metal pole at the top and the bottom. The lower pole is important to add weight to the wall hanging, helping it to hang better.

STEP 1

Cut the canvas to the required size, lay it out flat, and trace the fleur-de-lis motif at regular spacings all over the fabric, then draw little squiggles to fill the spacing in between.

STEP 2

Using a fine brush, paint artist's liquid frisket on to the motifs and squiggles. Leave this to dry and repeat with another layer so that the shapes are in relief. Again, leave this to dry.

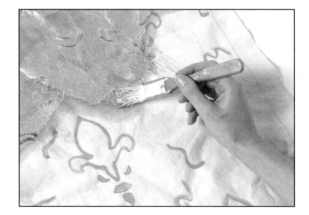

STEP 3

Paint a slightly thinned, oil-based gold paint over the canvas, leaving a 1-inch gap around the edge, and leave to dry completely.

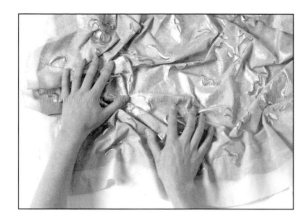

STEP 4

Once dry, scrunch up the fabric so that there are plenty of folds and creases.

STEP 5

In a well-ventilated room, spray a variety of strong blues and violets from different angles so that when you spread the canvas flat, the folds are different colors. Leave to dry completely, then lay the canvas flat under something heavy to even out for a few days before hanging.

This vibrant and shimmering wall hanging has raised motifs which give a three-dimensional appearance to the fabric, reminiscent of batik or tapestries.

DINING ROOM

MARQUETRY DINING TABLE

CHECKLIST

*golden yellow oil-based
    semigloss paint*

medium-size brushes

raw sienna artist's oil color

oil-based scumble glaze

mineral spirits

newspaper

large soft brush

pencil

string

card and craft knife

masking tape

burnt sienna artist's oil color

comb

burnt umber artist's oil color

rag

acetate and spray adhesive

black artist's oil color

fine artist's brush

satin polyurethane varnish

You don't have to search out and pay a small fortune for an expensive antique dining table in order to give your dining room an air of sophistication. This striking effect will transform and rejuvenate an old table and provide a focal point central to any good dinner party. If you don't have an old table or are reluctant to paint the one you have, your local lumber merchant will cut a piece of medium-density fiberboard to the required size and you can fix it on to an old base to create a new table.

Although in technical terms this project might be a bit more demanding than some of the others, it is well worth the extra effort and by following the steps closely, you will achieve a stylish and elegant finish that should last for years. You can easily adapt the design to suit a setting for four, six, or eight people, depending on the size of the top (and your dining room!) or if you prefer, reduce the design in size to fit a small occasional table.

If you are working on an old dining table, ensure that you key the surface sufficiently before painting. To do this, remove any wax with mineral spirits and fine wire wool; varnish should be sanded off with medium, then fine paper. When the surface is smooth and keyed, apply two coats of golden yellow oil-based semigloss paint as a base coat.

Though this finished surface will be more durable than an ordinary waxed table, it is advisable not to place hot objects directly on to the surface.

STEP 1
Mix a glaze of raw sienna artist's oil color, 50% oil-based scumble, and 50% mineral spirits and apply on to the surface. Crumple some newspaper into a ball and dab the wet glaze all over.

STEP 2
While the glaze is still wet, very lightly soften the effect by feathering over the surface with a very soft brush. Leave to dry overnight.

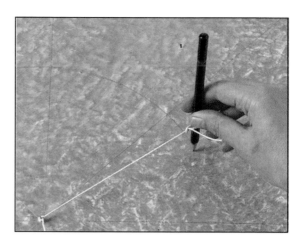

STEP 3
Mark a circle in the center of the table about 10 inches in diameter (this is for a 4-foot diameter table), using a pencil tied to a piece of string, nailed to the center.

STEP 4
Cut out a leaf-shaped template from stiff card. Working from the center circle, mark out a symmetrical pattern according to how many leaves you want to have and mask them off using low-tack masking tape.

STEP 5
Apply a mixed glaze of burnt sienna artist's oil color, 50% oil-based scumble, and 50% mineral spirits, inside the panel.

STEP 6
While this glaze is still wet, stipple it roughly with a long hard brush.

STEP 7

In the center of the table draw a star-shaped image lightly in pencil, then paint in the star using the same glaze.

STEP 8

Mask off a border around the edge of the top. Apply the burnt sienna glaze and drag a comb through it, working from the center outward. Leave to dry overnight.

STEP 9

Mark a line through the center of each leaf. Add a little burnt umber to the burnt sienna glaze to make it slightly darker, then apply to one half of each leaf and mottle it with a rag. Carefully remove the masking tape and leave to dry overnight.

STEP 10

Using the wreath template, stencil in the darker glaze around the center circle.

STEP 11

Carefully highlight the edges of the leaves using a fine artist's brush and some thinned black oil-based paint. This will hide the pencil lines.

STEP 12

Use the second wreath stencil to decorate the edge of the table. Leave to dry and protect with at least two coats of polyurethane varnish.

This striking table top uses golden-colored paints to replicate the look of expensive inlaid wood, but can be achieved using an old wood table or even medium-density fiberboard.

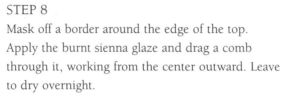

SWEDISH DINING CHAIR

CHECKLIST

light blue water-based paint

lilac water-based paint

medium-size brushes

burnt umber artist's oil color

mineral spirits

rag

steel wool

acetate and craft knife

spray adhesive

mauve water-based paint

fine artist's brush

I BOUGHT THIS CHAIR at an auction as part of a set of six, mainly because I liked the overall elegant classical shape. I was lucky that it was in such good condition, as second-hand chairs often suffer from neglect. It is advisable to check that they are solid and stable with no rickety legs or collapsible seats, and to look out for woodworm which is easily spotted if there are clusters of even holes over the surface.

The blend of colors used here combined with the gentle curves and overall shape of the chair gives a distinctly Scandinavian appearance. This look is usually known as "Gustavian," named after the Swedish monarch Gustav III who encouraged and apparently raised the standards of Swedish design in the late eighteenth century. The final appearance should have a pale, dusty, bluey-gray feel which looks slightly distressed and echoes the clean and simple lines of the period. The classical fabric used to cover the seat was chosen to complement both the elegant shape and the colors used on the chair.

Because this chair was in such good condition, the preparation needed wasn't too time-consuming. Initially, I smoothed over the surface with steel wool to remove any rough or damaged areas and to provide a key for painting. I then applied two thick coats of a very light-blue water-based paint, ensuring that I created lots of texture with heavy brushstrokes. Let this dry completely before going on to Step 1.

STEP 1
Dip the tip of an old rough brush into some water-based lilac paint and lightly brush it over the heavy paintwork to highlight the texture. Leave to dry for a few hours.

STEP 2
Mix a little burnt umber artist's oil color with some mineral spirits and, working quickly, brush over the chair. (If you can't work quickly, do this and the following step in sections.)

STEP 3
While the brown glaze is still wet, wipe most of it off with a rag; this will highlight more of the texture. Leave to dry overnight.

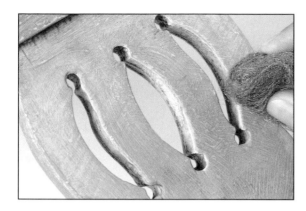

STEP 4

Rub selected details of the chair with steel wool to highlight more of the underlying colors.

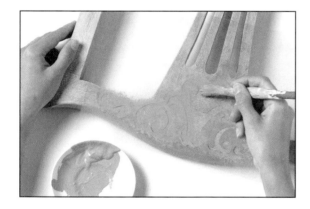

STEP 5

Fix the stencil in position with repositional adhesive spray. Stipple on a stronger blue color in water-based paint.

STEP 6

Highlight the design with a contrasting mauve color and a small artist's brush.

The finished chair has further embellishments in blue and mauve on the legs and around the edge of the seat, to echo the stenciled swirls on the chair back.

DISTRESSED FLORAL SIDEBOARD

CHECKLIST

pale blue water-based paint

medium-size brushes

masking tape

cream water-based paint

tissue paper

crackle medium

acetate and craft knife

spray adhesive

*pink, blue, mauve, and green
water-based paints*

rag

antique-pine beeswax

THIS OLD SIDEBOARD WAS in a very sorry and neglected state when I rescued it from an old building that was being renovated. It had been thrown on to a refuse dump by the builders who obviously considered it to be well past its usefulness. The many layers of paint were chipping away, it had a few deep gashes in the woodwork, and the original ball feet were falling off.

However, I thought it would be worth the effort to try to revitalize it because it was otherwise solid and sturdy and I had a feeling that it could end up as a pretty piece of furniture that would enhance a cottage-style dining room. To create a country theme, I chose a mixture of garden and wild flowers which I sketched and simplified to make the door panel stencils. The distressed effect was achieved by using a crackle medium together with an effect called frottage. This technique relies on materials like tissue paper to lift the glaze to create an interesting background texture.

Even when aiming to produced an aged effect, it is still important to invest some time and effort in preparation. In order to create a good solid base on which to work, I filled the cracks and holes then rubbed the whole piece down with medium, then fine sandpaper to provide a key on which to paint. I then applied two full coats of pale blue water-based mat paint as a base coat for the stenciling and crackle mediums.

STEP 1

Using low-tack masking tape, mask off a panel inside the doors and drawers and paint a cream water-based paint, thinned to the consistency of light cream, inside the panel.

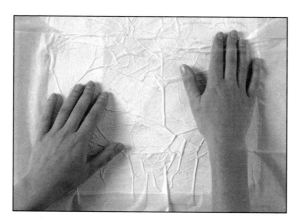

STEP 2

While this is still wet, gently lay a piece of tissue paper on to the surface and press it down firmly, ensuring that you keep the wrinkles in the paper.

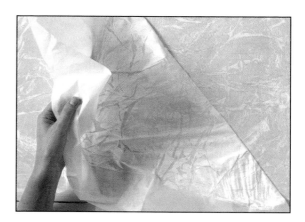

STEP 3

Carefully peel the tissue paper away to reveal a texture underneath and leave to dry completely.

STEP 4

Apply a water-based crackle medium to the surrounding areas (not in the center of the panels) and leave to dry completely.

STEP 5

Fix the basket of flowers stencil in the center of each panel and stipple the flowers and leaves in different shades of pink, blue, green, and mauve water-based paint.

STEP 6

With a dry brush, stipple a small amount of white paint over the various colors to soften them, creating a more subtle effect.

STEP 7

Once the image is completely dry, carefully peel away the flower stencil.

STEP 8

When the crackle medium is dry, apply a layer of cream water-based paint, working quickly, and ensuring that you do not go over the same area twice as this will lift the paint.

STEP 9

Carefully peel the masking tape away from the panels and let the whole object dry.

STEP 10

Once everything is dry and you're completely happy with the finished effect, apply an antique-pine beeswax over the whole object and leave for about a half hour, then burnish with a soft rag. This will protect the surface and add to the appearance of age.

New feet and handles as well as a country-style stencil and distressed treatment, have transformed this sideboard from an ugly piece of junk to a decorative item of furniture.

STUDY

PALE WOOD INLAY DESK

CHECKLIST

*cream oil-based semigloss
    paint*

medium-size artist's brush

*raw sienna, burnt sienna,
    and burnt umber artist's
    oil colors*

mineral spirits

oil-based scumble glaze

large dusting brush

large coarse brush

natural sponge

stiff brush

masking tape

off-white water-based paint

indelible black marker

rag

antique-pine beeswax

WHEN I ACQUIRED THIS black ash melamine desk from a friend, it was functional but bland and uninteresting, more suited to an office than a home. I saw it as a bit of a challenge to transform it into a still workable but more stimulating piece of furniture.

I decided upon a paint finish that would simulate the appearance of inlaid polished hardwood, because it is a traditionally appropriate look for an object or piece of furniture that might be used in a study or library. To create a realistic and subtle wood effect, it is important to have the right set of tools to soften, shuffle, sponge, and drag the glaze. The black and white "stripes" are easily created with white paint and a black marker, to simulate expensive ebony and ivory inlays.

Before I set about painting the desk, I added an upstand to the top and a bit of decorative molding around the bottom in order to give it a more substantial look. It was then rubbed all over with medium-grade sandpaper, followed by fine cabinet paper, to give the melamine a key; this helps to provide a surface on which subsequent layers of paint will adhere.

As a base for the wood effect, I painted the whole desk with a layer of oil-based creamy semigloss paint, let this dry overnight, then smoothed over the surface with fine cabinet paper. I then wiped down the surface with a damp rag and repeated the treatment with another coat of the creamy paint.

STEP 1
Mix a little raw sienna artist's oil color into a glaze with 50% mineral spirits and 50% oil-based scumble and apply to the surface. While the glaze is still wet, paint on thick and thin uneven stripes of color with burnt sienna and burnt umber. Remember it is easiest to work in sections, for example a side or drawer, before the glaze dries.

STEP 2
Using a soft dusting brush, very gently soften and blend the effect.

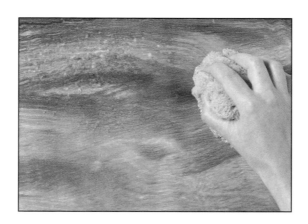

STEP 3
While the surface is still wet, take a coarser brush and "shuffle" it down through the glaze to create a slightly grained effect.

STEP 4
Dip the edges of a damp natural sponge into a little mineral spirits and very lightly dab patches of the surface. Be careful not to overdo this.

STEP 5
Create a grained border surround to frame this effect by dragging a stiff brush to within 1½ inches of the edges. Leave to dry completely.

STEP 6

Using low-tack masking tape, mask off a
¼ inch wide space for the inlay effect at the edge
between the dragged surround and the inside
panel. Apply an off-white water-based paint evenly
inside the space and leave to dry for a few hours.

STEP 7

Using an indelible black marker, make diagonal
strokes over the white panel as neatly as you can.

STEP 8

Carefully remove the masking tape to reveal the
mock inlay effect.

STEP 9

When all the paints and glazes are dry, and you're
completely happy with the resulting effect, add
the finishing touch by applying an antique-pine
beeswax and burnishing with a soft cloth. As well
as protecting the surface and creating a soft sheen,
this will tone down the white of the mock inlay to
reflect an ivory color.

From bland office desk to sophisticated study bureau,
using paints to create an imitation hardwood with a
mock ivory and ebony inlay.

MALACHITE WINE TABLE

CHECKLIST

- *emerald green oil-based semigloss paint*
- *medium-size brushes*
- *oil-based scumble glaze*
- *viridian green artist's oil color*
- *raw umber artist's oil color*
- *French ultramarine blue artist's oil color*
- *cheesecloth*
- *card*
- *mineral spirits*
- *gold paint*
- *fine artist's brush*
- *gloss polyurethane varnish*

MALACHITE IS A SEMIPRECIOUS mineral which is often found in its polished state as jewelry, ornaments, and art objects. Traditionally, it has also been used as a source of green pigment and would have been mixed with linseed oil and applied to canvas with a knife.

I have always been inspired and excited by the purity and intensity of color in natural substances like malachite and although small and quite intricate, I felt that this little wine table would benefit from a finish that is bold and decorative. The deep greens are reminiscent of a traditional gentleman's study, a room which was often used as a retreat in order to enjoy a quiet drink away from the rest of the household.

This paint effect is not as difficult to recreate as it looks, but it is always useful to take inspiration from the stone itself, either by visiting a museum or a gem store.

Initially, the whole table was smoothed over with wire wool and two coats of emerald green oil-based semigloss were applied as a base coat for the malachite, leaving the object to dry overnight. As a decorative finish, mock malachite is particularly suited to small items but remember it is easier to work on objects with a flat surface. As a final step, it is essential to apply at least three coats of high-gloss oil-based varnish to complete the effect. Not only will this protect the surface, but it will also enhance the impression of polished stone.

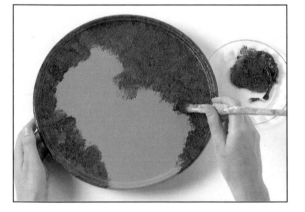

STEP 1
Stipple over the surface a thick even layer of viridian artist's oil color mixed with a little oil-based scumble glaze.

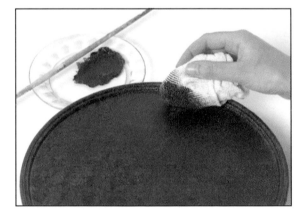

STEP 2
While the previous layer is still wet, gently dab on small patches of raw umber and French ultramarine blue with a piece of cheesecloth. Blend the colors a little with the green, to create a subtle even texture.

STEP 3
Start with a larger piece of card and pull it through the glaze to create jagged circular patterns, wiping the excess paint from the card as you go.

STEP 4

Continue by making more detailed patterns with a smaller piece of card.

STEP 5

Thin the remaining viridian green mixture with a little mineral spirits and apply to the legs. Mottle with a soft cloth and leave to dry for a few days.

STEP 6

As a final touch, pick out areas of detail in gold.

A polished-looking malachite finish brings this small, traditionally shaped wine table to life, creating a distinctive feature for a gentleman's study.

MAPLE FILE CABINET

CHECKLIST

*cream oil-based semigloss
   paint*

medium-size brushes

raw sienna artist's oil color

oil-based scumble glaze

mineral spirits

large soft brush

fine artist's brush

black oil-based paint

satin polyurethane varnish

ALTHOUGH A SMALL CHEST of drawers like this could be used in almost any room, I immediately saw it transformed with a paint technique that would sit perfectly in a study or home office. It is quite functional and ideal for storing files and stationery.

The combination of the faux maple effect and handpainted black edges echoes the Biedermeier style, which embodied strong proportions and light-colored wood veneers with ebonized inlays. This was a nineteenth-century style of art and furniture which has had an enormous influence on interior designers and architects, particularly in Europe and America. Its attraction for me is that it can be applied on a grand scale or used to give substance to a small piece of furniture like this. The technique would also look good applied to a desk or a lamp base.

Although this faux maple technique requires a bit more concentration and ability than some of the other projects, it is worth the effort to achieve a finish that is timeless and classical. You may wish to practice the technique first, using a prepared piece of board, or look at maple finishes on period furniture for inspiration.

Before you begin the steps, prepare the cabinet by applying a base coat of cream oil-based semigloss paint and leave to dry overnight.

STEP 1
Make a thin glaze consisting of raw sienna artist's oil color mixed with 30% oil-based scumble and 70% mineral spirits. Apply on the cabinet and shuffle a stiff brush through it to create a broken dragged effect.

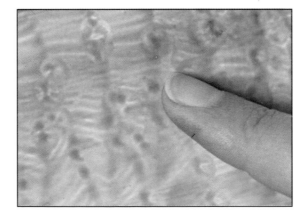

STEP 2
While this is still wet, make little puddles of glaze by gently pressing your finger on to the surface to create random patterns.

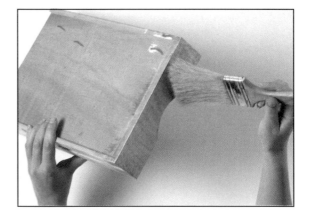

STEP 3
Using a very soft brush, lightly soften the effect by feathering the surface. Be careful not to overdo this and leave to dry overnight.

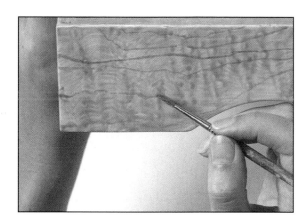

STEP 4

Paint in fine grain lines in raw sienna artist's oil color using a fine artist's brush. Leave to dry completely overnight.

STEP 5

Paint in black edges to the drawers in oil-based paint by masking off thin edges. Leave to dry, then protect with a coat of satin polyurethane varnish.

Faux mapling creates an understated and stylish look for any piece of furniture, and is ideal for a working home office where it will blend in well with other wood furniture—traditional or modern.

BEDROOM

CHECKLIST

cream oil-based semigloss paint

medium-size brushes

yellow ocher artist's oil color

mineral spirits

oil-based scumble glaze

rag

blue-gray water-based paint

fine artist's brush

acetate and craft knife

spray adhesive

lilac and pink water-based paints

SILHOUETTE HEADBOARD

THE IDEA OF USING a silhouette image had appealed to me for years, but I could never find the right application for it until I saw this bedstead at an auction. I immediately decided that the curved profile was perfect for an illustrative image surrounded by stenciled details.

To prepare the headboard, I used a varnish remover to take off the many layers that had been applied over the years. Always be careful when using varnish and paint removers; wear gloves and a face mask for protection.

Why not personalize the project with your own silhouette? To create the template, I took a photo of my seven-year-old daughter in profile, then after having it processed and working directly onto the print, I carefully filled in the outline shape of her face with a black marker pen. I then photocopied and enlarged the image to the required size using a photocopier. I sprayed the back of the copy with repositional adhesive and placed it onto a cutting board. On top of this and overlapping the image by about an inch, I masked a piece of acetate on top and carefully cut out the silhouette using a sharp craft knife. The oval shape for the background was copied from a large plate I have at home and reduced in size. The surrounding garland stencils add a decorative touch to the final effect.

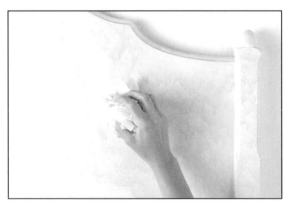

STEP 1
Prepare the headboard with a base coat of cream oil-based semigloss. Once this is dry, apply a glaze of yellow ocher artist's oil color mixed with 50% mineral spirits and 50% oil-based scumble, and dab it with a rag to create a mottled effect.

STEP 2
When the yellow glaze is completely dry, pick out areas of detail around the top and edges of the headboard in a soft blue-gray water-based paint using a fine artist's brush.

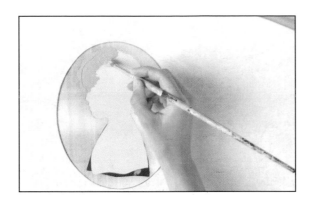

STEP 3

Mark the oval of the silhouette on to the headboard, apply the blue-gray paint, and leave to dry thoroughly. Place the silhouette stencil in the center of the oval and stipple in a pale lilac color.

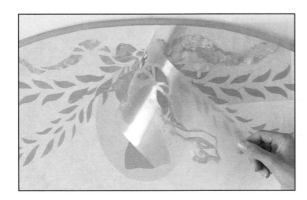

STEP 4

Using a variety of soft blues and lilacs, enhance the silhouette image by surrounding it with stencils of leaves and bows.

STEP 5

Pick out selected smaller areas in a contrasting pink with a fine artist's brush.

This finished version of the headboard has been painted in slightly more vibrant tones of blue and lilac. Experiment with mixing your own colors to create the right subtle shades to complement your bedroom color scheme.

DECOUPAGE CHEST OF DRAWERS

CHECKLIST

white water-based semigloss paint

medium-size brushes

black and white photocopied images

craft knife

spray adhesive

watercolor paints

fine artist's brush

polyurethane varnish

burnt umber artist's oil color

rag

large soft brush

mineral spirits

crackle medium

lavender water-based paint

IN ITS NATURAL STATE, this small chest of drawers was uninteresting and uninspiring. The oak was badly stained and dented so I decided on a paint treatment that would be quite decorative in the hope that it would end up as a pretty chest of drawers that could be used at the side of a bed or as a small dressing table.

Decoupage is a good way of cutting corners and getting illustrative images on to furniture and accessories without actually having to draw them on freehand. It is an effective way to add interest to an otherwise plain background and is an ideal finishing touch because the variety of images you can use is almost endless—from magazines and wrapping paper, to greetings cards and wallpaper. Unlike traditional decoupage, this project relies upon using photocopied black and white images,

so that by adding a bit of color with a small artist's brush and a set of watercolors, you have the flexibility of tying the project into an existing color scheme and perhaps providing an interesting focal point.

Using a crackle medium is a good way to provide more interest on furniture, incorporating two colors—white underneath showing through as cracks, and lavender as the main colour – as well as creating added texture to the surface.

Before embarking on the steps, I prepared the surface of the chest of drawers by smoothing over with sandpaper to remove an old peeling varnish. I then applied a base of two coats of white water-based paint and left it to dry overnight.

STEP 1
Spray the back of your photocopied image with spray adhesive and carefully apply to the surface, smoothing out any wrinkles with a soft rag.

STEP 2
Use artist's watercolor paints and a fine brush to apply thin layers of different colored washes to the leaves and flowers.

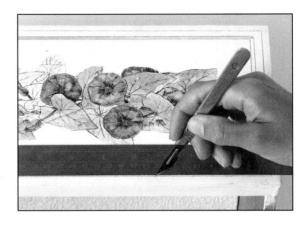

STEP 3
Mark out a thin border around the edges and carefully score along the lines with a sharp knife.

STEP 4
Paint a thin wash of gray inside the lines which have been scored. This will help to create crisp edges and straight lines to frame the images.

STEP 5
Again using a small artist's brush, paint a contrasting red wash around the edges. Leave to dry completely.

STEP 6
Seal the whole chest of drawers with one even coat of polyurethane varnish and leave to dry.

STEP 7

Rub on an antiquing glaze of burnt umber artist's oil color mixed with a little mineral spirits.

STEP 8

Remove the excess glaze with a rag and dust over with a soft brush, leaving only enough to create a patina of age. Leave to dry overnight.

STEP 9

Cover the entire casing in a crackle medium and leave to dry completely. Carefully paint on a lavender water-based paint and wait for the cracks to appear.

STEP 10

Leave the entire chest to dry completely overnight. Then apply a polyurethane varnish tinted with a little burnt umber artist's oil color to enhance the aged appearance.

The combined use of modern crackle mediums and traditional decoupage images decorated with watercolor paints, adds color and interest to an otherwise worn and plain chest of drawers.

STENCILED CLEMATIS WARDROBE

CHECKLIST

*white oil-based semigloss
    paint*

medium-size brushes

mineral spirits

oil-based scumble glaze

yellow ocher artist's oil color

rag

*pink, blue, and yellow
    water-based paints*

acetate and craft knife

spray adhesive

fine artist's brush

satin polyurethane varnish

THIS OLD WARDROBE HAD been left lying around my workshop for so long that I had stopped seeing it as a piece of furniture. I had been using it to store paint and brushes until a friend remarked on its appealing shape and good proportions.

In its original pine state, ideally the wardrobe would have been treated with a bit of liming or antique-pine beeswax, but two of the panels had been replaced with poor quality veneers and it was covered in paint spills and old varnish stains. So I decided on a paint finish in soft pastel colors which would enhance its shape and hide any shortcomings in the quality of the wood.

To give a bit of interest to the shape of the wardrobe, I added a length of thick baseboard around the bottom edges to give it a more solid base. The dents and cracks were filled, and the surface was rubbed over with coarse, medium, and fine sandpaper before two coats of white oil-based semigloss paint were applied as a base for the yellow glaze.

I emphasized the shape of the doors by ragging the center panels and dragging the surrounds. By using the templates you can add as little or as much detail to a piece of furniture like this as you like and it now makes an ideal focal point for a bedroom.

STEP 1
Mix a glaze of yellow ocher artist's oil color with 50% mineral spirits and 50% oil-based scumble, adding a teaspoon of white oil-based semigloss. Apply the glaze in the center panels and dab gently with a soft rag to create a mottled effect.

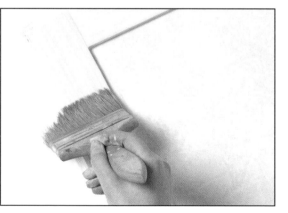

STEP 2
Working quickly before the glaze dries, apply to the surrounding areas of the doors and drag a stiff brush through the glaze starting with the horizontal, then the vertical panels. Repeat this on the sides and top of the cabinet.

STEP 3
Using the clematis stencil, stipple on light water-based colors in pink, blue, and yellow.

STEP 4

Stencil a ribbon across the top of the doors in a light blue water-based paint.

STEP 5

Thin the blue paint with a little water and pick out and enhance small areas of detail with a small artist's brush. Finish and protect the wardrobe with a coat of satin polyurethane varnish.

The delicate flowers trailing down the sides of this wardrobe add a soft touch to an otherwise solid piece of furniture. The success of this project relies upon using a subtle range of colors for the stenciled leaves and flowers.

FOLK ART BEDSIDE CABINET

CHECKLIST

lavender water-based paint

medium-size brushes

acetate and craft knife

spray adhesive

terra-cotta and green water-based paint

medium-grade sandpaper

burnt umber artist's oil color

polyurethane varnish

mineral spirits

rag

steel wool

THIS TIRED AND WORN old cabinet was given to me by a friend of mine who refused to see any potential in it at all. However, I liked its proportions and knew that it would not take long to give it a new personality simply by adding a few offcut moldings around the door and around the base.

Small cabinets like this are cheap and commonplace in second-hand shops and as long as they are an interesting shape and are in sound condition, they make ideal low-cost projects for beginners. I decided that a folky rustic feel would be an appropriate look for this cabinet to complement a country-style bedroom, with some very simple stencils and a few aging techniques.

The first step was to begin by smoothing over the surface using medium-, then fine-grade sandpaper to get rid of the existing rough paintwork, and to key the surface to be painted.

Next, I applied a very thick coat of water-based lavender paint, ensuring that I created lots of heavy brushmarks on the surface. This texture is important for this paint technique when you come to the stage of rubbing the aging glazes into the surface. The brushstrokes will help to create a depth and interest which could not easily be achieved on a smooth surface, and add to the rustic appearance. Leave this base coat to dry thoroughly overnight.

STEP 1
Stencil the flower and leaves in terra-cotta and green water-based paints in symmetrical patterns around the object. Thin these two colors with a little water, paint washes of color onto the moldings, and leave to dry.

STEP 2
Use a medium-grade sandpaper to lightly rub away at the stenciled patterns and at the corners of the object to give it a worn look.

STEP 3

Mix some burnt umber artist's oil color with polyurethane varnish and a little mineral spirits and brush over the entire object.

STEP 4

While the varnish is still wet, remove as much of it as you can with clean rags until you are left with an aged patina effect. Leave to dry completely.

STEP 5

As a finishing touch, burnish the surface with fine steel wool, paying particular attention to moldings and corners.

A very simple stencil can create an instant country-style piece of furniture with decorative borders, given a faded and aged appearance using sandpaper and steel wool.

BATHROOM

MARBLED TROMPE-L'OEIL PANELED SCREEN

CHECKLIST

*white oil-based semigloss
    paint*

medium-size brushes

gray artist's oil color

oil-based scumble glaze

mineral spirits

rag

natural sponge

masking tape

yellow ocher artist's oil color

feather

large soft brush

toothbrush

fine artist's brush

gloss polyurethane varnish

MARBLING IS A TECHNIQUE which takes a bit more thought and imagination than other paint effects. Basically, there are two types of marbling. To achieve the appearance of the real thing, it helps if you apply the technique on to an object or surface which might traditionally have been carved or composed in slabs of marble. It is also important to have a reference of some kind of the type of marble you wish to imitate. Avoid trying to copy the marble directly, but instead try to capture the general appearance, overall markings, and color subtleties.

The other, easier but not so convincing, method is to aim for a pleasant general marbling effect, which while attractive, does not attempt to be a realistic copy. On this screen I used a combination of these two methods. The two main colors, yellow and gray, are softer than the stronger yellows and grays you might find in a real marble like Siena, but the marks and effects achieved do reflect the real thing.

To achieve a truly effective marbled look, it is essential to work on a smooth non-absorbent surface. I began by priming the surface, then applying a coat of white oil-based semigloss paint as a base. When dry, I smoothed the surface with very fine cabinet paper and repeated with another coat, sanding it again when dry.

STEP 1
Mix a light gray paint into a glaze of 50% oil-based scumble and 50% mineral spirits and apply unevenly all over the screen.

STEP 2

While the glaze is still wet, mottle it all over with a rag or piece of crumpled newspaper.

STEP 3

Dip a damp sponge lightly into some white spirit and gently and sparingly use this to break up the wet glaze. Be careful not to overdo this. Leave to dry overnight.

STEP 4

Mark out panels about 2 inches inside the edge of the screen and use low-tack masking tape to mask off the areas.

STEP 5

Mix a glaze of yellow ocher artist's oil color with 50% oil-based scumble and 50% mineral spirits with a spoonful of white oil-based paint. Apply in patches inside the panels.

STEP 6

Mix a slightly darker gray glaze and apply to the patches in between the yellow glaze, then mottle the whole surface with a soft rag.

STEP 7

Disperse the wet glaze gently with a damp sponge dipped lightly in white spirit.

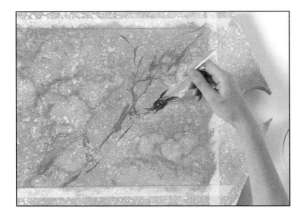

STEP 8
Mix some gray paint and some yellow ocher each with a little mineral spirits. Dip a feather into each color and drag across the surface to create veins.

STEP 9
Before they dry, soften some of the veins gently with a large soft brush. This will help to achieve depth to the overall effect.

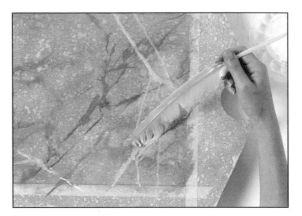

STEP 10
Use a feather to create sharper white veins with oil-based white paint and also spatter some of this color on to the surface with a toothbrush.

STEP 11
Carefully remove the masking tape from around each edge to reveal the marbled panel. Leave to dry thoroughly overnight.

STEP 12
Highlight the top and one edge of the panels with a fine artist's brush and some off-white paint thinned with a little mineral spirits. Create a shadowed effect on the other side and bottom of the panel with a darker gray thinned paint.

STEP 13
Leave to dry completely, then protect and enhance the entire screen with two coats of gloss polyurethane varnish.

Second-hand screens are hard to find, but it is easy to create your own from three hinged pieces of medium-density fiberboard. This surface is also ideal for marbling, as it is already very smooth and therefore needs little preparation.

CRACKLED MIRROR FRAME

CHECKLIST

crackle medium

medium-size brushes

yellow and mauve
 water-based paint

green water-based paint

off-white water-based paint

acetate and craft knife

spray adhesive

fine artist's brush

mineral spirits

polyurethane varnish

burnt umber artist's oil color

toothbrush

THIS IS A FINE EXAMPLE of what can be achieved with a little imagination, a few moldings, and some offcuts of wood. I measured an old mirror that had lost its frame and built a new one around it by gluing the offcuts together. Because these contoured moldings already had a charm of their own, I decided on a simple paint treatment which relies mostly on technique and involves minimal painting skills.

There are many ways to achieve the popular cracking and peeling paint effect used here. Some good art suppliers and decorator's merchants sell ready-made crackle mediums that work very well and are simple to use, but they can be expensive to buy and sometimes difficult to find.

If you cannot find some to buy in a store or would rather experiment with your own recipes, use liquid gum arabic which produces large cracks (this can be bought at most good art suppliers) or instead try using a very thick mixture of wallpaper paste which produces smaller cracks—or if you want to experiment, mix the two together! You will find that the size of the cracks and the texture created depend upon the proportions of the mixture and on how thickly you apply the top layer of paint. It may be wise to test your mixture first before applying it to the mirror frame.

When you are happy with the final result, it's important to varnish the surface, not only to protect against wear and tear, but to lessen the effects of damp.

STEP 1
Apply a base coat of yellow water-based paint and leave to dry. Apply a crackle medium and once it is dry, quickly apply a contrasting mauve water-based paint. Leave to dry for a few hours.

STEP 2
To soften the effect, apply a thin wash of off-white water-based paint thinned with about 30% water and leave to dry.

STEP 3
Stencil the garland shape in green and make small leaf marks using a fine artist's brush with a lighter and darker green. Leave to dry for a few hours.

STEP 4

Mix a tinted varnish with about 40% mineral spirits, 60% polyurethane varnish, and a squeeze of burnt umber artist's oil color. Apply to the frame, rubbing in hard into the corners of the moldings until it acquires an antiqued look.

STEP 5

Spatter random areas of the frame with brown speckles using a toothbrush dipped in the brown varnish. When the paints are dry, protect the surface with two coats of polyurethane varnish.

As an additional touch before you add the varnish, enhance the contours and moldings of the mirror frame, as here, by picking out selected areas using gold paint.

TORTOISESHELL TOWEL RAIL

CHECKLIST

cream oil-based semigloss paint

medium-size brushes

raw sienna artist's oil color

oil-based scumble glaze

mineral spirits

burnt sienna and raw umber artist's oil colors

newspaper

alizarin crimson artist's oil color

black oil-based paint

gloss polyurethane varnish

TOWEL RAILS, POPULAR DURING the Victorian era, were and are extremely serviceable pieces of furniture. Most of the older examples which are still intact can be quite expensive, but cheap reproductions are plentiful and can be found in second-hand shops or bought new in home furnishing stores. You can shop around for a pleasing design and with a swift and effective paint treatment like this transform it into a decorative piece of furniture that will complement your bathroom.

It's very quick and easy to get excellent results with this tortoiseshell finish, which makes it ideal for a first project. However, if you are unfamiliar with glazes, varnishes and their drying times, it is advisable to apply each step in sections at any one time, rather than attempt the whole object in one go.

There is no need to stick to traditional colors—this technique can be applied in a varied choice of colors so that you can tie it in with an existing color scheme. Or you may wish to apply the effect throughout your bathroom, for instance to a mirror frame, a bathroom cabinet, or a lavatory seat, for a coordinated look.

In order to prepare the towel rail for the paint effect, I first smoothed it over with steel wool, then applied two coats of cream oil-based semigloss paint as an initial base on which to work.

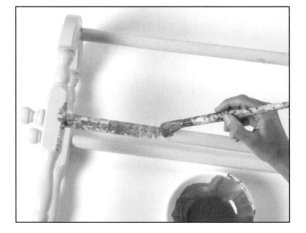

STEP 1
Mix a glaze of raw sienna artist's oil color with 50% oil-based scumble and 50% mineral spirits and apply all over the towel rail.

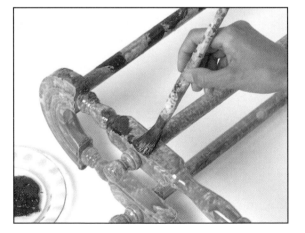

STEP 2
While the glaze is still wet and working quickly, apply patches of burnt sienna artist's oil color mixed with a little mineral spirits.

STEP 3
Using a slightly smaller brush, apply smaller patches of raw umber artist's oil color mixed with a little mineral spirits.

STEP 4

Crumple a piece of newspaper into a ball and mottle the effect all over. Leave to dry completely.

STEP 5

Use a little alizarin crimson and a very small amount of black artist's oil color to tint some polyurethane gloss varnish and apply two coats evenly over the entire towel rail.

The traditional tortoiseshell finish makes this rail a useful item in many rooms: for holding dish towels and oven gloves in the kitchen or for tidying clothes in the bedroom.

PANELED VANITY UNIT

THIS ORDINARY-LOOKING VANITY unit can easily be transformed into a decorative focal point if you want to give your bathroom a sleek and stylish look. Similar melamine units can be bought in home improvement centers and although they don't cost much, they are quite solid and highly functional when assembled from their flat-pack state. However, it is important to key the melamine surface, before painting, by abrading it lightly with fine glasspaper. Follow with an application of universal primer and a coat of oil-based semigloss paint.

Although this decorative marbled paneling effect might look daunting at first, it is actually quite simple to achieve. To make the process easier, don't attempt to mask off different sections and marble them separately. Instead, create an overall marbled effect, let it dry overnight, and then create the paneled look by masking off selected areas of your design and applying a tinted varnish. These varnishes are semi-transparent and let some of the underlying marbled effect glow through, creating a feeling of depth and movement.

The marbled surface was created first, as a base to work on. To do this, follow the steps for the Marbled *Trompe L'oeil* Screen, using as your colors burnt sienna artist's oil color mixed with white oil-based semigloss paint. To complete the look, consider carrying the effect around the bathroom walls, below dado rail height.

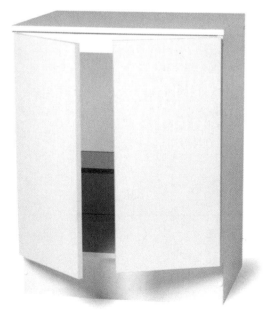

STEP 1
Once the marbled surface is dry, use low-tack masking tape to create a variety of geometric shapes. Mix a spoonful of white oil-based semigloss paint with some polyurethane varnish and apply inside the largest spaces. Dab with a rag to remove any excess.

STEP 2
Add a tiny drop of black oil-based paint to the remaining white-tinted varnish to make gray and paint inside the surrounding spaces. Rag off any excess glaze.

STEP 3

Tint a little polyurethane varnish with black oil-based paint and apply to the center diamond and corner spaces. Once again, dab with a rag to remove any excess.

STEP 4

Using a toothbrush, flick some of the white, gray, and black tinted varnishes lightly over the surface to create more interest.

STEP 5

Gently remove the masking tape and leave to dry before protecting with two coats of gloss polyurethane varnish.

This stunning paneled marble vanity unit has been finished with porcelain door handles and a Victorian-style sink set into the top. The diamond pattern has been designed to echo the tiled floor in this bathroom.

RUMPUS ROOM

TREASURE CHEST TOY BOX

CHECKLIST

pink water-based paint

medium-size brushes

light brown water-based paint

heartgrainer

fine artist's brush

acetate and craft knife

spray adhesive

black water-based paint

satin polyurethane varnish

A GOOD-SIZE TOY box is essential in a child's room. They are ideal for storage and for hiding bulky toys and games out of sight when attempting to tidy up. However, finished or painted boxes can be expensive to buy and might not always match your planned or existing color scheme. Why not keep an eye out for an old box that you can transform yourself? Not only are old wooden chests easy to find, they come in all sorts of shapes and sizes.

This simple project shows you how to rejuvenate an old and well-worn box into a fun and useful storage item which could also be used as a seat with a few cushions. This box had lost its lid, so I had to create one out of a piece of medium-density fiberboard, attached with

sturdy hinges to the back of the chest. The real hinges were then disguised with the stenciled hinges. Although I chose bold colors to create this chest, the end result would work just as well using soft pastel colors or if you have a distinctive color scheme already, consider duplicating the colors on your wallpaper or fabrics. There is no need to stick to traditional wood colors.

Because this chest was in such a delapidated state, the surface had to be keyed with medium, then fine sandpaper to remove flaking bits of paint and general roughness. I then applied two coats of a dirty-pink water-based paint as a base coat before the light brown graining color was applied.

STEP 1
Thin some light brown water-based paint with water to a consistency of heavy cream and apply to the surface, a side at a time.

STEP 2
While the glaze is still wet, drag a heartgrainer horizontally through it to make the graining marks. Leave to dry.

STEP 3

Mix a darker brown water-based glaze and paint uneven lines around the box with a fine artist's brush, to create the appearance of planks of wood.

STEP 4

Stencil on dark hinges around the corners and on top of the chest in a water-based paint. Leave to dry overnight and protect with at least two coats of satin polyurethane varnish.

The finishing touch on this pirate-style treasure chest is the exaggerated keyhole shape, which can be painted at the front of the box—even if your box doesn't have a real keyhole.

WEATHERED NAUTICAL DESK

CHECKLIST

dark blue water-based paint

medium-size brushes

white water-based paint

large brush

acetate and craft knife

spray adhesive

potato

red water-based paint

ruler

fine artist's brush

acrylic varnish

THIS DISHEVELED OLD school desk was yet another cheap and cheerful junk store find. Normally I wouldn't paint anything pine if it is in a reasonable condition; a good rub over with beeswax to bring out the warmth of the wood would be enough.

In this case, the desk had been put together using different types of wood and it looked a bit shabby. Its charming shape makes it perfect for a paint treatment and after deciding on a nautical theme, I set to work creating a weathered blue background for the nautical stamps and stencils. Because of its poor condition, I had to invest some time filling and sanding before applying a dark blue water-based base coat. This treatment is ideal as a shortcut if you don't want to spend hours bleaching and stripping old paint from an object.

This is an excellent project for adults and children to get involved in—children will love stamping on the little boats—but please supervise the young when sharp craft knives are involved. Armed with stencils and potato stamps, you can add as little or as much detail as you like. The white rope stencil acts as a framework for the little red and blue sailboat stamps. This theme could easily be continued around the room creating a wonderful seafaring frieze.

STEP 1
Paint a layer of white water-based paint thinned with 50% water on to the dry, dark blue base coat.

STEP 2
While this is wet and using a dry brush, rub and distress this glaze to create a milky weathered look and leave to dry.

STEP 3

Use the rope template to stencil a white border around the desk and along the top of the drawers.

STEP 4

Carefully cut a potato in half and carve sailboats in different sizes. Stamp them on to the desk in pale blues and bright reds.

STEP 5

Using a ruler, a fine artist's brush, and some thinned red water-based paint, frame the image and join up the ropes with a red line. Leave to dry and protect with at least two coats of acrylic varnish.

Seafaring themes are always popular with children, and they can help to decorate their own piece of furniture with with these simple sailboat stamps, ready-cut from a potato by an adult.

ABSTRACT BLACKBOARD

CHECKLIST

blackboard paint

*pastel pink, blue, green, and
    yellow water-based paints*

black water-based paint

medium-size brushes

acetate and craft knife

spray adhesive

acrylic varnish

THEY SAY THAT NECESSITY is the mother of invention, so when I couldn't find a suitable blackboard for my two small children, I decided to make one myself. The appeal of making your own blackboard is that it can be made in any size and the shapes and colors you use can be adapted to suit a variety of themes and ages.

My local lumber merchant cut out the abstract-style frame in medium-density fiberboard, using a template which I supplied. Fiberboard is ideal for projects like this because it is easily available and comes ready to paint. Another piece was cut out for the blackboard, which was fixed to the back of the frame. This was covered with blackboard paint, which can be bought at most good decorator's merchants, and is designed specifically for blackboards, creating a mat, easy to wipe surface when dry. One of the joys of working on children's furniture is the almost limitless scope you can have with color and pattern. Whether you choose bright and happy primary colors for a bold dramatic effect or soft pastel colors to achieve a more gentle subtle feel, you are sure to enjoy the experience enormously. These bold designs were inspired by the abstract leaf shapes on a Matisse painting, but I decided to use pastel colors to complement the children's existing rumpus room.

The duster was created from a small piece of stuffed felt, tied with wool, and knotted to a piece of wooden doweling. The doweling was fixed to a hole drilled into the blackboard frame.

STEP 1
Paint a pastel pink water-based paint over the frame. Leave to dry, then apply another coat.

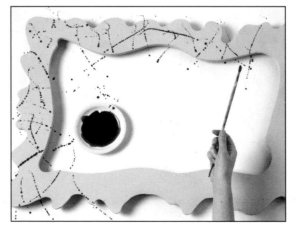

STEP 2
Thin a little black water-based paint and flick splashes over the whole frame. Leave to dry.

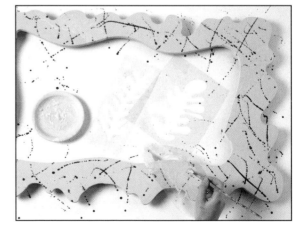

STEP 3
Using the first leaf-shape stencil, stipple in a blue water-based paint, positioning the stencil at random around the frame but leaving spaces for the other colors.

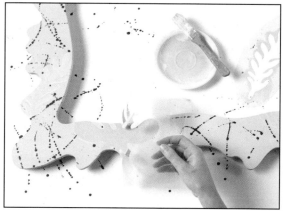

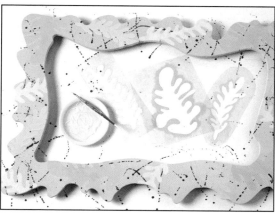

If you can't find the right item of furniture, remember you can sometimes create your own. This customized blackboard looks expensive, but was created cheaply from two pieces of wood, decorated simply with stencils and splattered paint.

STEP 4
Use the second leaf shape template to stencil in a soft pastel green.

STEP 5
Fill in any remaining spaces by stenciling the third shape in yellow. Leave to dry and protect with at least two coats of acrylic varnish.

SPATTERED SEASIDE CHAIR

CHECKLIST

*cream oil-based semigloss
    paint*

*black, pink, and green
    oil-based paints*

mineral spirits

toothbrush

carrot

craft knife

fine artist's brush

polyurethane varnish

THIS MUST BE ONE of the easiest items of furniture to obtain. Second-hand chairs can be bought individually or in sets in junk and thrift shops, garage sales, and auctions and are ideal for a variety of paint techniques.

This project shows you how to transform an ordinary looking chair into a unique and colorful piece of furniture for a child's room. There are no limits to the colors you can use, but it helps to be influenced by something existing in the room such as the curtain fabric or bed covers. In this case, the seat cover was a source of inspiration, evoking a seaside theme. I highlighted small sections in pink, which brought out the chair's turned legs and grooved details.

It is always a good idea when working on children's furniture to keep the techniques simple and quick. Apart from growing up and out of trends and themes, children tend unintentionally to abuse things so it helps if you can revitalize an object with very little effort. Stamping and splattering are also techniques which children will enjoy doing themselves, especially as it is quick and easy to produce excellent results.

*No special tools or paints are needed to create this simple
but charming chair, which can be decorated using common
household items—a carrot and an old toothbrush.*

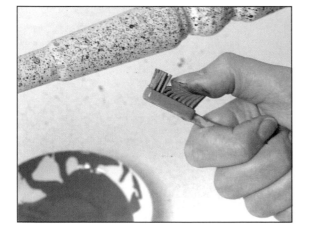

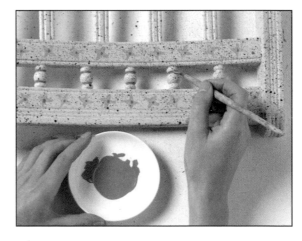

STEP 1
Apply a base coat of cream oil-based semigloss paint and leave to dry. Spatter black, then pink oil-based paint (thinned a little with mineral spirits) using a toothbrush. Leave to dry overnight.

STEP 2
Using a sharp craft knife, cut little star shapes into a carrot. Brush a pale green oil-based paint on to the cutout shape and stamp across the back frame of the chair.

STEP 3
Pick out areas of detail on the back frame and legs of the chair using a fine artist's brush and some thinned pink oil-based paint. When the paints are dry, protect with two coats of polyurethane varnish.

MUSICAL GRANDDAUGHTER CLOCK

CHECKLIST

white oil-based semigloss
*   paint*

medium-size brushes

decorator's liner paper

ruler and indelible black
*   marker*

pencil

spray adhesive

masking tape

taupe water-based paint

acetate and craft knife

light blue water-based
*   paint*

fine artist's brush

satin polyurethane varnish

gold paint

burnt umber artist's oil color

large brush

toothbrush

THIS OLD GRANDDAUGHTER clock was a great pleasure to work on and because of its lovely shape and beautiful chime, it was easy to decide on an effect that would enhance its charm.

It was given to me by a watchmaker friend as a gift for my two small daughters and after he had reassured me that it had no antique value, I happily set to work preparing it by smoothing it over with medium-, then fine-grade sandpaper, before applying two coats of white oil-based undercoat. This style of granddaughter clock is not unusual; you are likely to discover similar clocks at auctions, antiques stores, and the better quality junk dealers.

The music sheet idea was inspired by the clock's chime which strikes the hour and half hour and has a deep resonance. If you don't feel able to draw the musical notes yourself, you can photocopy pages from old musical scores and enlarge or reduce them to the required size before sticking them on to the object.

Not all clock cases are appropriate for painting and it is important that you make sure of any item's value by consulting an expert before you begin painting. In this instance, the old casing was damaged and had previously been stained a dark oak color which I felt was inappropriate for a child's room, so I had no qualms about painting it to achieve a lighter more pleasing effect.

STEP 1
Cut a sheet of decorator's liner paper to the required size and using music scores as a guide, copy the notes with a ruler and black indelible marker. Pencil and cut out a curve on each corner of the music score, using a cup as a guide.

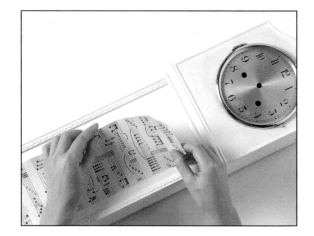

STEP 2
Glue the back of the paper with spray adhesive and carefully stick it into position, pressing down firmly on to the center of the clock.

STEP 3
Draw and mask off panels with low-tack masking tape. Paint the inside of the panel with a taupe water-based mat paint. Leave to dry.

STEP 4
Using the violin template, stencil in a light blue water-based paint.

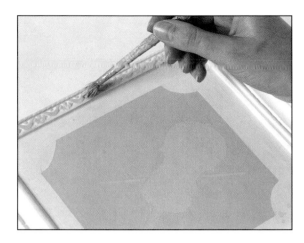

STEP 5
Using the same blue paint, pick out any areas of detail and moldings with a fine brush.

STEP 6
Using a ruler and a fine artist's brush, paint a fine blue line around the music scores to frame them.

STEP 7
Mix a slightly darker blue water-based paint and with a fine brush outline the violin shape and paint in the details. Leave to dry.

STEP 8

Using a soft brush, seal the whole object with an even coat of satin polyurethane varnish and leave to dry.

STEP 9

Highlight any metal details and other small selected areas of the clock face using gold paint and a fine artist's brush.

STEP 10

Mix a little burnt umber artist's oil color with satin polyurethane varnish and apply to the whole object. Rub and distress this with a dry brush, taking off any excess as you do this.

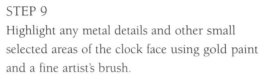

STEP 11

Mix a little more of the burnt umber with the satin polyurethane varnish and flick specks of this on to the clock at random, to enhance the already yellowed and aged appearance. Let the object dry overnight, then apply two coats of satin polyurethane varnish over the whole surface.

The tinted varnish gives a warmth and instant aging to this musical-themed clock, and also tones down the harshness of the white paint. The music score idea can of course be adapted and applied to any item as decoupage.

KITCHEN

CHECKLIST

*white oil-based semigloss
    paint*

medium-size brushes

masking tape

pencil

*pale blue oil-based semigloss
    paint*

fine artist's brush

pink oil-based paint

crackle varnish

burnt umber artist's oil color

mineral spirits

cotton balls

satin polyurethane varnish

CRAQUELURE COUNTRY DRESSER

THIS OLD KITCHEN CABINET was found in a thrift shop. Originally, these cabinets were built with a lower cupboard (which this one had been parted from) and had a worktop which could be pulled out from between the two upper and lower halves of the cabinet. Although it looked shabby and dated, I could envisage it in a country farmhouse setting, painted in rustic earthy colors and surrounded by dried flowers, stenciled walls, and wooden plate racks. I was encouraged to renovate it by the recent trend toward unfitted furniture in kitchens. Freestanding utility cabinets are fashionable again due to their adaptability because you can rearrange them as you please, easily redecorate them as your color scheme changes, and take them with you when you move house.

I chose soft earthy colors and a technique known as craquelure to give this postwar cabinet a lived-in country feel. To complete the look, I replaced the top two center panels with wire netting backed with fabric and substituted attractive wooden knobs for the cracked plastic handles. The wire was covered with decorator's filler mixed with white water-based paint, and rubbed over with the aging glaze. As a base, the dresser was first given a coat of white oil-based semigloss paint.

This is an ideal way to create your own custom-made kitchen on a tight budget, by gathering together individual pieces of furniture like this over a period of time. The possibilities are endless and each piece will have its own distinctive charm.

STEP 1
Mask off insert panels on the doors and drawers with low-tack masking tape. Paint a light pastel shade of blue in oil-based semigloss paint inside the panels. Leave to dry overnight.

STEP 2
Carefully remove the masking tape and paint a fine line in pink oil-based paint around the panels to highlight them.

STEP 3

Follow the instructions supplied with the crackle varnish and apply the two coats at appropriate intervals—usually two hours between coats. Leave to dry, avoiding a damp or humid room.

STEP 4

Apply an aging glaze of burnt umber artist's oil color mixed with a tiny drop of mineral spirits. Work in sections—a door or panel at any one time—gently covering an area.

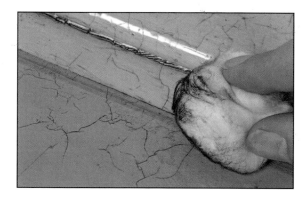

STEP 5

Wipe over with cotton balls to remove excess glaze and to highlight the crackled effect. Leave to dry overnight and protect with two coats of polyurethane varnish.

The warm rustic colors and crackled surface of this dresser are perfectly suited to a country farmhouse kitchen. Complete the look with door panels backed with gingham or floral fabric.

MOSAIC BREAKFAST TABLE

CHECKLIST

cream water-based paint

medium-size brushes

large rutabaga

craft knife

*blue, green, and orange
   water-based paints*

satin polyurethane varnish

metallic-silver spray paint

black water-based paint

stiff brush

THE QUIRKY AND LIVELY technique used to transform this old and delapidated kitchen table is so easy to execute and can be done on almost any scale and applied to a variety of objects. By cleverly using some basic household items like a craft knife, a large rutabaga or potato, and some bright Mediterranean water-based colors, you can create an imitation mosaic effect that when varnished is hard-wearing and practical—and therefore ideal for the kitchen.

The appeal of this finish is its imprecise pattern and the illusion of texture achieved by the freehand manner in which you stamp the various colors. An infinite variety of designs, shapes, and sizes can be created and it is the ideal technique to experiment with by using favorite images as inspiration. There is no limitation as to how detailed to make your own pattern, but the color combinations you use are important, so experiment with these beforehand on a piece of prepared board or card. As you can see with this table, using a colorful and imaginative paint technique can enliven even the plainest item of furniture, with no apparent redeeming features, into a desirable object.

To prepare the table for the mosaic effect, I first sanded the surface thoroughly and applied two coats of cream water-based paint to the top and legs as a working base coat.

STEP 1
Cut a large rutabaga in half with a sharp craft knife, then score deep ridges in a grid shape to create roughly symmetrical squares.

STEP 2
Using separate brushes for each color, brush blue and green water-based paint unevenly on to the square shapes.

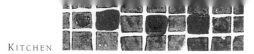

STEP 3

Carefully place the rutabaga on to the surface and press down firmly, repeating until the whole area is covered. Leave to dry.

STEP 4

Cut a single square shape from another piece of rutabaga and brush on a bright orange water-based paint. Stamp on top of the blue-green pattern in selected areas to create a focal point. Leave to dry and apply two coats of polyurethane varnish.

STEP 5

Spray the table legs all over with metallic-silver paint. When dry, rub in a little black water-based paint and distress it with a hard brush to create a metallic-pewter effect.

To add a bit more interest to the table, a couple of pieces of decorative wood trim were attached as an arch between the two sets of legs. Here the pewter effect has also been applied to this matching chair.

DISTRESSED WINE CABINET

CHECKLIST

burgundy water-based paint

dark green spray paint

medium-size brushes

acetate and craft knife

spray adhesive

lime-green, dark blue, and white water-based paints

fine artist's brush

medium-grade steel wool

antique-pine beeswax

WINE RACKS, ALTHOUGH THE most convenient way for storing wine, are usually quite dull and uninspiring. This being the case, I decided to have a go at making my own cut-price piece of furniture from old junk and bits and pieces I had lying around the workshop.

I started from scratch, using an old cabinet with the door removed, as a basic framework to house the bottle rack. I fitted together a standard wooden assembly wine rack, gluing each piece of wood together, and securing the whole frame inside the cabinet. Inspired by the trend for butcher's blocks, I added a practical solid pine top as a useful kitchen work surface, and treated it with many layers of antique-pine beeswax. For a bit of added interest, staircase spindles sliced in half were attached to the sides and moldings were added to the base.

The colors and design were naturally enough inspired by the subject itself. I painted the whole outside of the cabinet in deep burgundy as a suitable background for the stenciled blue and red grapes and lime-green vine leaves. The inside of the cabinet, including the wine rack, was sprayed with dark green paint to match the bottles. Using a spray paint was the quickest way to reach all the intricate corners of the rack. As a final touch, I rubbed over the whole item of furniture with a couple of coats of antique-pine beeswax to add to the distressed and aged appearance.

STEP 1
Stencil the vine leaves and stalk in a lime-green water-based paint on to the sides of the cabinet.

STEP 2
Continue by stenciling the grapes in a deep blue water-based paint and leave to dry.

STEP 3
Dip the tip of a dry brush in white paint and lightly touch the blue to create a frosted look.

STEP 4

Remove the stencil and using a fine brush and the lime green paint thinned with a little water, enhance the stalk and paint smaller tendrils to create more interest.

STEP 5

Lightly rub over the paintwork to distress it slightly with medium-grade steel wool.

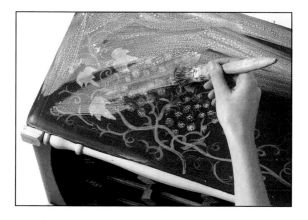

STEP 6

Thin some white water-based paint with about 70% water and brush over the entire cabinet rubbing it in to give a milky appearance. Leave this to dry and apply an antique-pine beeswax over the whole cabinet to age it.

Even old items lying around the home can be recycled into distinctive decorative objects, with a bit of imagination. A paint treatment is also the ideal way to disguise different types and ages of wood, if you are customizing junk.

GRANITE-EFFECT COUNTER

CHECKLIST

white oil-based semigloss paint

medium-size brushes

natural sponge

black oil-based semigloss paint

pink-purple incandescent paint

acetate and craft knife

spray adhesive

gold paint

gloss polyurethane varnish

THIS GRANITE-EFFECT PAINT technique is ideal for beginners and is probably one of the easiest and quickest treatments you can do. It is a versatile effect as well, because it can be applied to almost any smooth surface and although the desired effect here is polished granite, you can vary the end result by using different color combinations to suit your own interior scheme. Because gray is a neutral color it works with most things, however, and the weighty granite appearance of this counter would sit well in most styles of kitchen, whether modern or traditional. You can always add a bit more interest and frame the effect by stenciling an image around the counter.

If you are working on a surface which is already in your kitchen, ensure that you cover the surrounding areas with newspaper attached with masking tape. It is also important to remove all food products before you begin to work.

This is an easy and instant way to rejuvenate your kitchen without going to the trouble of redecorating a host of cabinets and other items. Make sure you protect the finish with at least two coats of gloss polyurethane varnish, and although the surface will then be reasonably hardwearing, it is advisable to avoid putting extremely hot items on to the counter.

STEP 1
Apply a white oil-based semigloss base coat and leave to dry overnight. Sponge on an even pattern using mid-gray semigloss. This color can be mixed by adding a little black to the white semigloss.

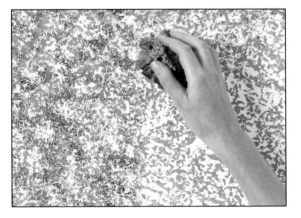

STEP 2
Add a bit more black to this mixture to make it a darker gray color and again sponge it evenly all over the surface.

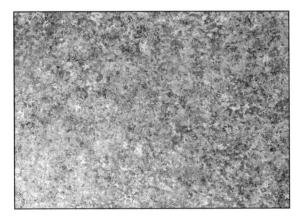

STEP 3
Add some of the white semigloss to the mixture to make a light gray and again sponge evenly all over the surface and let the surface dry overnight. Apply a layer of pink-purple incandescent paint to give the surface an added reflective quality.

STEP 4

Using the Greek key template, stencil the image in black about 1½ inches from the edges of the top all the way around to create a border. Remove the stencil and leave to dry completely.

STEP 5

Place the same stencil back on the image but move it a fraction so that it does not register exactly and stencil in the gold paint. This will create a three-dimensional image. When it's dry, protect with two coats of gloss polyurethane varnish.

A distinctive counter can very easily be created with some simple sponging techniques. The additional layer of incandescent paint adds a special sheen to the finished kitchen surface.

SOLARIUM

GOLD LACE WICKER TABLE

CHECKLIST

vinegar

rag

spray adhesive

lace pattern

gold spray paint

dark green water-based paint

gold paint

fine artist's brush

exterior varnish

THIS VINTAGE WICKER TABLE was tired and weather-beaten when I recovered it from an old barn. After bringing the wicker back to life with some color, I wanted to try something simple but decorative on the glass top and decided on a spray and stencil effect. This treatment is an easy and instant decorating technique for creating a repeat pattern or one-off motif on to glass. The same technique can also be used on furniture and walls with a bit more planning and thought.

I decided to use lace as a template for my design because I wanted something quite intricate, but simple to apply. You can buy panels of lace from remnant and fabric stores; search for a pattern that is relevant to the size of your table (for smaller objects try a doily). If a piece of lace you like is too small or you want to design your own pattern, join pieces together or mask off unwanted sections with newspaper.

Spray paints are a convenient way of applying color through delicate images like this. They dry very quickly, are durable, and can be applied to almost any surface. It is important not to over-spray; build up gradually in thin even layers, letting each coat dry in between.

It is important to fix the glass top back on to the table with the sprayed image face-down. This will prevent the pattern from being scratched.

STEP 1
Remove the glass and clean it with a rag dipped in vinegar. When it is dry, spray the underside evenly all over with repositional adhesive.

STEP 2
Position the lace pattern carefully on to the glass, ensuring that it is in the center. Press it down on to the surface, smoothing out any wrinkles.

STEP 3
Apply the gold spray lightly and evenly over the entire lace pattern.

STEP 4

Carefully remove the lace to reveal the pattern on the glass and leave to dry for a few hours.

STEP 5

Paint the wicker base of the table in a dark green water-based paint and leave to dry. Use a fine artist's brush to pick out areas of detail with gold paint mixed with a little mineral spirits. Protect with a coat of exterior varnish.

Old wicker can turn gray and shabby with age and the effects of the weather. Rejuvenate it with this bold green and gold treatment, complemented with a delicate gold lace glass top.

TROMPE-L'OEIL STONE PEDESTAL

CHECKLIST

fine builder's sand

cream, green, and gray water-based paints

medium-size brushes

natural sponge

masking tape

STONE ORNAMENTAL FURNITURE can be quite expensive, but you can easily imitate the real thing using clever paint techniques. This solid-looking pedestal was actually made from six ½-inch-thick medium-density fiberboard panels, which were cut to shape at the local lumber merchants. I glued and pinned them together, then added a bit of baseboard around the bottom and molding around the top to make a more interesting shape.

Because fiberboard is so smooth, in order to create some texture I mixed a small amount of builder's sand (this is available from most hardware stores) with the water-based base coat to a thick creamy and gritty consistency before applying it to the pedestal.

It is important when trying to achieve an uncontrived natural look like this to use an absorbent, mat water-based paint for the base coat and to let this dry completely. As you apply subsequent thinned-down glazes, they will sink in and dry at different times, and as you work and rub these glazes in, you will create a natural-looking effect. The combination of colors you choose, however, are essential for a realistic effect and it is the build-up of the layers of glaze which produces depth and movement as well as texture.

As a final touch, I added the *trompe-l'oeil* highlights and shadows in order to create a three-dimensional appearance to the mock stone effect.

STEP 1
Mix some sand with cream water-based paint and apply the mixture unevenly over the entire surface. Leave to dry overnight.

STEP 2
Make a transparent wash by mixing 50% gray water-based paint with 50% water. Brush over the object in uneven patches and leave to dry.

STEP 3
Repeat this step with a moss green wash made in the same proportions, and again leave to dry.

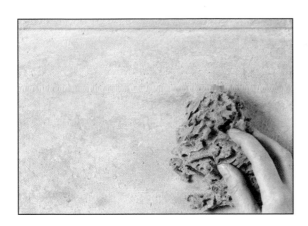

STEP 4

Sponge on moss green water-based paint unevenly over the surface using a natural sponge.

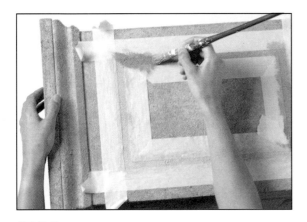

STEP 5

Mask off a panel 1 inch wide for the *trompe-l'oeil* effect. Stipple an off-white water-based paint on the left side and top panel, and a darker gray-green color on the bottom and right panel.

Even smooth surfaces can be given the appearance and texture of stone with the help of paint mixed with a little sand. The trompe-l'oeil panels add to the deception by creating an illusion of sculpted stonework.

VERDIGRIS GARDEN CHAIR

CHECKLIST

gold spray paint

medium-sized brushes

turquoise water-based paint

rag

*light green and off-white
    water-based paints*

black water-based paint

toothbrush

wood glue

exterior varnish

THIS TYPE OF CAST-IRON GARDEN chair is reasonably inexpensive to buy and can be found in many garden centers. Because of its sprayed white factory-finish, it was crying out for a paint technique that would add to its charm, letting it blend into the natural colors of a garden or solarium setting.

The overall shape and intricate details make it ideal for a faux metallic finish such as verdigris, which would instantly age the chair, giving it an air of faded grandeur. As a paint technique, verdigris is one of those unpredictable treatments that can end in different results each time you apply it, but it's an ideal effect to experiment with because it's relatively easy.

The aim is to emulate the natural result of condensation on metals such as copper, bronze, and brass. Over time, this condensation produces beautiful blue and green powdery deposits which, although highly toxic, have historically been used as pigments for artist's colors. The versatility of this technique lies in the fact that you can choose from a range of base colors from brass and copper to different shades of gold, and it is an effective way to lend an air of substance to a new object.

The chair can be protected against the elements for use in the garden, by sealing the finish with a water-based wood glue thinned with water, followed by a few coats of exterior varnish.

STEP 1
Spray gold over the whole chair and leave to dry. Apply a turquoise water-based paint over the entire object, working the brush well into the details.

STEP 2
Immediately wipe the excess paint off with a rag, revealing the gold base coat in places. Leave to dry for a few hours.

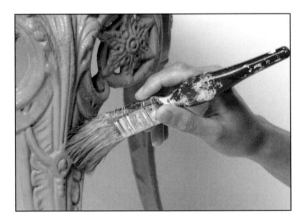

STEP 3
Apply another coat with a light green color and immediately wipe off again with a rag. Leave the surface to dry completely.

STEP 4

Thin an off-white water-based paint with 20% water and brush this all over the surface, again rubbing back with a rag in places to reveal areas of underlying color.

STEP 5

Spatter random patches of flecks, using a toothbrush dipped in thinned black paint. Seal the surface with wood glue thinned with 30% water, and protect with two coats of exterior varnish.

A verdigris paint effect is the ideal way to instantly antique modern garden furniture and, as with the real effect, the technique will always produce slightly different results, so a set of chairs will each have their own individual look.

TEMPLATES

USE THESE TEMPLATES FOR each of the named projects in Part 1, and you can also use them for your own designs. Please note that some projects use more than one template. Reduce or increase the size of each template using a photocopier, scaling up or down according to the size of the object you are working on.

LAPIS LAZULI COFFEE TABLE
(pages 36–7)

SWEDISH DINING CHAIR
(pages 50–51)

FLOATING MARBLE & GILDED CONSOLE TABLE
(pages 30–33)

GRANITE-EFFECT COUNTER
(pages 102–3)

STENCILED OCCASIONAL TABLE
(pages 42–3)

LAPIS LAZULI COFFEE TABLE
(pages 36–7)

STENCILED OCCASIONAL TABLE
(*pages 42–3*)

MARQUETRY DINING TABLE
(*pages 46–9*)

RIGHT:
STENCILED OCCASIONAL TABLE
(*pages 42–3*)

SWEDISH DINING CHAIR
(*pages 50–51*)

FLEUR-DE-LIS WALL HANGING
(*pages 44–5*)

DISTRESSED FLORAL SIDEBOARD
(pages 52–5)

MARQUETRY DINING TABLE
(*pages 46–9*)

SILHOUETTE HEADBOARD
(*pages 64–5*)

SILHOUETTE HEADBOARD
(*pages 64–5*)

STENCILED CLEMATIS WARDROBE
(*pages 70–71*)

SILHOUETTE HEADBOARD
(*pages 64–5*)

STENCILED CLEMATIS WARDROBE
(*pages 70–71*)

FOLK ART BEDSIDE CABINET
(pages 72–3)

CRACKLED MIRROR FRAME
(pages 78–9)

WEATHERED NAUTICAL DESK
(pages 86–7)

TREASURE CHEST TOY BOX
(pages 84–5)

ABSTRACT BLACKBOARD
(pages 88–9)

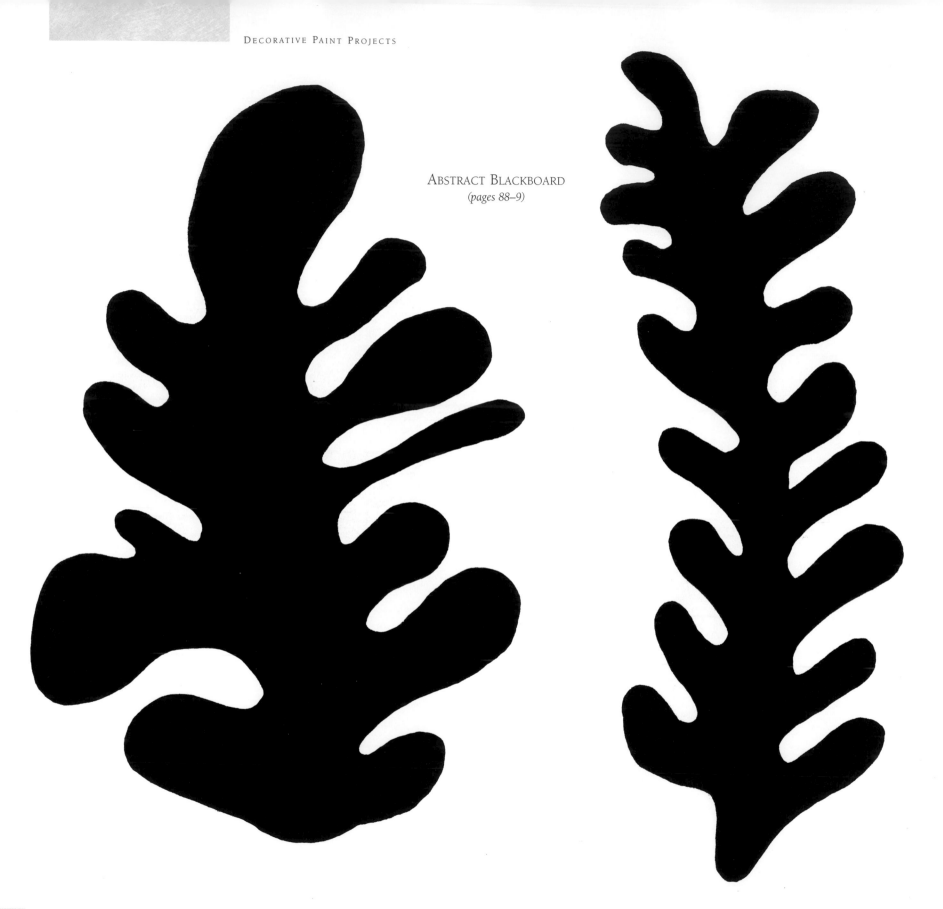

ABSTRACT BLACKBOARD
(pages 88–9)

DISTRESSED WINE CABINET
(*pages 100–101*)

MUSICAL GRANDDAUGHTER CLOCK
(*pages 92–5*)

PART 2
ACCESSORIES

FABRIC

CARNATION & TULIP TABLECLOTH

CHECKLIST

fabric paints in primary colors and white

natural sponge

acetate and craft knife

spray adhesive

medium-size brushes

fine artist's brush

THERE IS AN ABUNDANT CHOICE of plain tablecloths in linen stores and unless they are finely decorated, they don't cost much to buy. This makes them ideal for a simple and effective stenciling project like this. You can apply this technique to a large or small tablecloth by adapting the stencils and reducing or enlarging them to the appropriate size.

In terms of a theme, the possibilities are endless. You could have a celebratory theme, for example, with balloons and toys for a child's birthday party or make it festive with holly and ivy. All you have to do is photocopy the images you want to use, reduce or enlarge them to size, and trace them on to stencil acetate. In this case, I decided to divide the tablecloth into folded segments which would produce eight place settings. This also made it easier to position the flower templates, and the green stenciled leaves around the edge helped to create a border.

The fabric paints I used are available in a wide range of colors from art and fabric stores. To create an interesting palette, I would suggest mixing the stronger colors with white to produce softer pastel shades.

STEP 1
Use a natural sponge to apply a pale cream fabric paint over the entire tablecloth.

STEP 2
Once the first sponged color is dry, apply a slightly deeper beige color to create a textured background and leave to dry.

STEP 3
Stencil leaves around the edge of the cloth in a light blue-green color. Remember to spray the back of the stencil lightly with adhesive to hold it in place on the fabric. Leave to dry.

STEP 4

Fold the tablecloth into eight segments and stencil the carnation with red petals and green stems on every alternate segment.

STEP 5

Pick out details and highlights of the carnation with white, using a fine artist's brush.

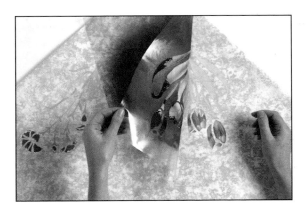

STEP 6

In the alternate spaces which are left, stencil the tulip with blue petals highlighted with white, and stipple in green stems.

A plain white tablecloth can be transformed with bunches of tulips and carnations for each place setting, surrounded by a delicate border of leaves. Sponging adds an instant background color for the stencils.

MATISSE-INSPIRED PILLOWS

CHECKLIST

soft pencil

red, blue, and green fabric paints

medium-size artist's brush

gold relief fabric paint

THIS WAS A PROJECT I particularly enjoyed and when I was asked to spice up some plain pillow covers, I had no hesitation about what to do with them.

For as long as I can remember, I have been inspired by the paintings of Henri Matisse, the French painter who helped revolutionize painting at the turn of the century. His use of stunningly vibrant colors and bold simplified shapes was influenced by Islamic mosaics and his paintings have a timeless quality. They are an ideal source of inspiration when searching for simple bold images and good color combinations, which is what I have tried to achieve on these pillows.

In order to make them bright and happy, I have used bold primary fabric paint colors which are designed to be used on fabric without spreading or bleeding out when washed. The gold relief fabric paint is available in tubes from artist's suppliers.

The completed pillow makes a bold statement when scattered along with others of the same design but in different colorways and would help to lift any room lacking in a bit of color. If you make a number of different-style removable covers, you can cheaply and easily change the mood of a room simply by changing your pillow covers.

STEP 1
Lay the pillow cover out flat and mark out the design lightly with a soft pencil.

STEP 2
Apply the red fabric paint with a medium-size artist's brush and outline the floral shapes. Leave the cover to dry.

STEP 3
Use a gold relief fabric paint and squeeze it around the inside and outside of the red shape. Again, leave to dry.

Freehand painting need not necessarily rely upon a great deal of artistic ability. These pillows are stunning because of their painted simplicity and bright colors, using basic childlike flower shapes.

STEP 4

Fill in the whole of the background with the blue fabric paint and leave to dry.

STEP 5

For the finishing touch, paint the inside of the flowers with bright green fabric paint.

CANVAS FLOOR CLOTH

CHECKLIST

*white, peach, green, blue,
    red, lilac, and terra-cotta
    water-based paints*

medium-size brushes

natural sponge

masking tape

acetate and craft knife

spray adhesive

satin polyurethane varnish

THE IDEA FOR THIS painted canvas rug springs from canvas floor cloths which were used from the late eighteenth century onward in both Europe and America. These were commonly found in country homes and were generally made from heavy-duty canvas covered in painted backgrounds and stenciled patterns and then sealed with many layers of varnish.

Commonly thought of as the forerunner of modern linoleum, these floor cloths not only provided a solution to cold and hard floors, but were also very hardwearing and easy to clean and their popularity continued until well into the late nineteenth century.

Apart from the advantage of being able to create your own unique design and one that enhances your interior decor, these easy-to-clean painted rugs can be adapted to be used over floorboards and in kitchens and bathrooms. They could also be used as robust wall hangings.

It is important to use at least a medium-weight canvas which can be bought from a good artist's supplier or fabric store. Cut it to the size you want, then stretch it on to a piece of flat board or a large table using masking tape to secure the sides. Having done this, apply two thick coats of white water-based paint as a base and leave to dry.

STEP 1
Mask off a border about 2 inches from the edges, using low-tack masking tape. Using a natural sponge, apply peach, then green, then light blue in soft colors, keeping within the center of the masked-off area. Leave to dry.

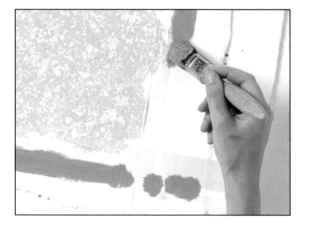

STEP 2
Mask off another border creating a thin line ½ inch thick and paint a lilac water-based paint carefully in between the masked-off lines and leave to dry.

STEP 3
Position the classical urn template in the center of the lower half of the canvas and stencil in a warm terra-cotta color.

STEP 4

Stencil two lilies in the urn at different heights using stronger colors of blue, red, and green, moving and overlapping the stencils slightly to create a fuller effect.

STEP 5

Continue to stencil, adding the swirling border to the edge of the floor cloth. Apply at least three full coats of satin varnish to protect the paintwork, adding a little white to the varnish to soften the image slightly.

This finished floor cloth has been adapted in slightly warmer colors with additional painted borders, in order to complement the warm tones of the wood parquet flooring in this room.

CHERUB LAMPSHADE

CHECKLIST

white, green, pink, cream, and blue water-based paints

medium-size brushes

card, acetate and craft knife

spray adhesive

soft pencil

fine artist's brush

satin polyurethane varnish

burnt umber artist's oil color

THIS COMBINATION OF STENCILING and decoupage can be used to transform almost any small object or piece of furniture, but it is particularly useful for revitalizing old and unused fabric lampshades which can become faded or dusty. Even if you don't have any old shades lying around the house, they are quite easy to find and will not cost much in junk stores or garage sales.

This technique relies upon covering a fabric shade completely, rather than working with the fabric. It is an ideal technique for beginners to practice with, because the heavy brushstroke base coat means that any mistakes can just be painted out and started again. It is also an easy finish to adapt to your own color scheme and decor by using the same room colors, or instead of cherubs you could use images from leftover bits of wallpaper in the room where the lamp will be used. Failing that, you can use cut outs from pictures in magazines or bits of wrapping paper. The final coat of tinted varnish is essential to give an instant warmth and aging to the shade, tying in with the period feel evoked by the Victorian cherubs.

It is important to use low-wattage bulbs when lighting shades that have been painted in this way, otherwise the heat may affect the paints and varnish. However, this will have the advantage of casting a softer light, helping to create a more intimate atmosphere.

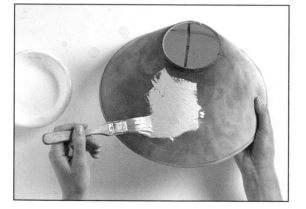

STEP 1
Prepare the shade by applying a thick coat of white water-based paint and leave to dry.

STEP 2
Divide the shade into six equal sections marking lightly with a pencil. Cut a piece of card as a template and draw scalloped curves around the top and bottom of each section.

STEP 3
Paint the scalloped shapes in a light green water-based paint, using a fine artist's brush, and leave to dry completely.

This Victorian cherub lampshade was inspired by the images on a sheet of traditional wrapping paper, decorated further with stencils and scalloped edges. A yellowing tinted coat of varnish adds to the period feel.

STEP 4

Cut out and glue on your decoupage images using spray adhesive, applying one to each section of the shade. Stencil the leaf border along the pencil line dividing each section, using a pale pink water-based paint.

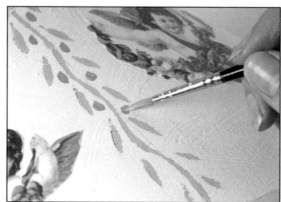

STEP 5

Using a fine artist's brush, highlight the edges of the scalloped shapes in a cream water-based paint thinned with a little water. With the same brush, edge the top and bottom of the shade with blue water-based paint.

STEP 6

Use the same brush and blue color to dot berry shapes between the stenciled leaves.

STEP 7

Tint some clear satin polyurethane varnish with a little burnt umber artist's oil color and apply two coats over the entire shade.

MISTY CLOUDS WINDOW SHADE

CHECKLIST

*sky blue, light and dark
   green spray paint*

card, acetate, and craft knife

spray adhesive

deep red oil-based paint

small stiff brush

THE BEAUTY OF WINDOW SHADES and semitransparent drapes is the effect which is created as the light passes through them. Because the intensity and quality of light will change as the day progesses, so will the design on the fabric change. Plain window shades are easy to find in home improvement centers and this project is a cheap alternative to those made from expensive fabrics.

This idea was originally inspired by the image of window boxes or flowerpots sitting on a windowsill. To ensure that the finished result gives a balance of sky and poppies, remember to unroll the window shade to match the length of your window before you start.

Spray paints are ideal for this project because you can create a misty cloudy background which is not opaque, but still has a reasonable permanence to light, which shouldn't fade over time.

Always remember to wear a face mask when using spray paints and to spray in a well-ventilated room. It helps to spread your window shade out on a large table or cleared floor area and give yourself plenty of room. Protect any surrounding areas with newspapers or old sheets as particles of spray tend to settle over a large area. Do not overspray, but build up the image gradually in light layers until you end up with the required effect.

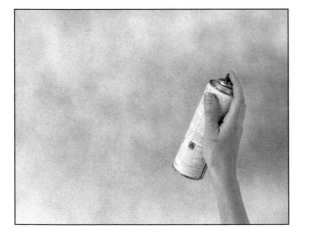

STEP 1
Spray a sky blue color lightly and unevenly on to the window shade, graduating the density of color from darkest at the top to becoming lighter two-thirds of the way down.

STEP 2
Starting from the lower edge, spray a light green color making it darker at the bottom and becoming lighter as you spray up, stopping about a third of the way up the window shade.

STEP 3
Cut out the cloud shapes from stiff card and use spray adhesive to fix them on to the window shade about two-thirds of the way up. Lightly spray over again with blue paint.

STEP 4

Using the poppy template, cut a stencil and place along the bottom. Cover the rest of the window shade to protect it, then spray over the stencil with a dark green color.

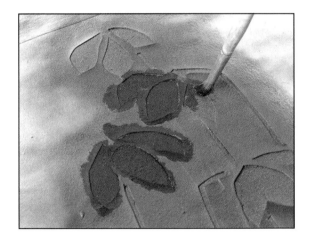

STEP 5

Use a small stiff brush to stipple on a deep red color in oil-based paint for the poppy heads. Ensure the window shade is completely dry before rolling back up ready to hang.

Spray paints are used carefully in gradual layers on this window shade to create a subtle misty effect, blending the sky and poppy images together.

GLASS

FROSTED HURRICANE LANTERN

CHECKLIST

acetate and craft knife

spray adhesive

synthetic sponge

frosting varnish

fine artist's brush

gold paint

THE HURRICANE LANTERN USED in this project is one of the few items which I already had in my home. Similar lanterns can be easily obtained in department stores and gardem centers, and fortunately the cheaper ones usually have plain glass, rather than tinted or patterned, so that you can customize them yourself. Most of the designs available are reproductions of eighteenth-century storm lanterns, but are mainly used these days to add an elegant touch to a dining table or to create a glow outside on a summer's evening.

For this simple technique, I decided to echo the theme of the sea, which is often associated with storm lanterns, with inspiration from shells, anchors, and starfishes. This is a straightforward paint effect; the main ingredient is a frosting varnish which can be bought in most good artist's suppliers and craft stores. It is important to use a synthetic sponge for this technique, rather than a natural one, in order to achieve the fine frosting effect. This frosting will create a wonderful glow when a candle is lit inside the lantern.

It's important to clean the glass thoroughly with diluted vinegar before you start. This will help the varnish adhere to the surface. Ornamental lanterns are usually made of thin glass, so do handle with care.

STEP 1
Cut out the starfish, anchor, and shell shapes from a sheet of acetate.

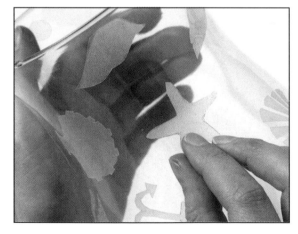

STEP 2
Apply a spray adhesive to the back of the shapes and carefully position them in an assorted pattern around the lamp.

STEP 3
Pour a little of the frosting varnish on to a plate and sponge it all over the object in an even layer. Leave it to dry for a few hours.

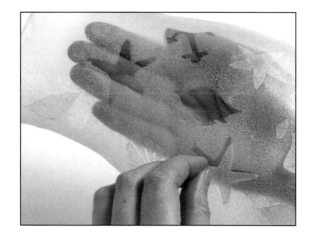

STEP 4

Once the frosting is completely dry, carefully peel away the shapes.

STEP 5

Using a little gold paint and a fine artist's brush, paint a fine line around the top and bottom of the glass lantern.

Often the most stylish treatments are also the simplest. The classical shape of this hurricane lantern has been enhanced with an elegant sponged frosting and decorated with gold edges to match the base and candleholder.

LACE FLOWER VASE

CHECKLIST

metallic-gold paint

masking tape

fine patterned lace

spray adhesive

white spray paint

fine artist's brush

THIS IS A WONDERFUL technique for transforming almost any glass object simply and cheaply, although it does require a bit of patience and delicate handling.

The soft shape and curves of this glass vase makes it ideal for a treatment as refined as this, but it is essential to find a piece of lace with a very fine delicate pattern and small shapes. The hardest part of this project is trying to manipulate the lace carefully around the vase, so a repositional spray adhesive is essential. This helps the lace to stay firmly in place around the object, otherwise the sprayed color would bleed underneath and look messy. The trick is to end up with a sharply defined image all over.

You needn't follow the colors I have used here—why not experiment on offcuts of glass (but tape off the sharp edges first for safety) to see what effects can be achieved when using a mixture of colors together? It is important to use spray paints, however, because of their adhesion to glass and quick-drying qualities. Remember to build up the color in light, even layers; do not attempt to spray a thick coat all in one go, otherwise you may end up with a runny mess.

Before you start the project, it is important that you clean the glass thoroughly with neat vinegar and ensure that the surface is completely dry before applying the lace and spray paint.

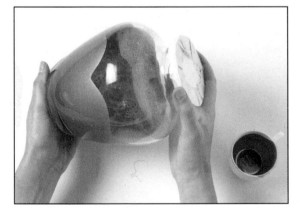

STEP 1
Pour some metallic-gold paint into the vase and mask the top off to prevent it leaking out. Swirl the paint around until the inside is covered and pour out any remaining paint. Leave to dry overnight.

STEP 2
Spray one side of the lace pattern with repositional spray adhesive and gently place it around the vase pressing it firmly onto the glass, and securing it around the neck with an elastic band.

STEP 3
Holding the vase carefully so as not to disturb the lace, spray on an even layer of white paint.

STEP 4

Before the white spray dries, carefully remove the lace and leave to dry completely for a few hours.

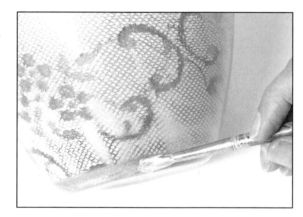

STEP 5

Using the same metallic-gold paint as before, paint a thin border around the top and bottom of the vase with a fine artist's brush.

A stenciled pattern doesn't necessarily have to be created from a template. This gold vase relies on a section of lace as a stencil, which is ideal for wrapping around a curved object and is an easy way to create a lot of instant detail.

TULIP STORAGE JAR

CHECKLIST

card and pencil

masking tape

medium-size artist's brush

imitation lead tube

glass paint in blue, red, and yellow

ALL HOMES RELY ON storage containers to keep the kitchen or workroom tidy and this basic storage jar can be found in most cookshops, or you can use an old coffee jar for this project if you don't want to buy a new container.

This plain jar was transformed into a rich and vibrantly colored decorative item by using a faux stained glass technique. This is achieved by using imitation lead and glass paints, which are available from artist's suppliers and craft stores. These paints should be applied with care, as they dry very quickly and it is also not possible to rectify mistakes by painting them out, as with conventional paints. A shelf lined with a variety of colored jars like this would create a stunning focal point of interest in any home. Although you could apply almost any type of design, I decided on something quite simple in the form of a stylized tulip with leaves. The beauty of a technique like this really lies in the purity and translucency of the colors as the light pours through the glass, bringing the colors to life.

Storage jars are also an ideal starting point to practice on because of their size and easy handling. Once you feel confident enough with the material, you can move on to more ambitious and complex glass painting projects. For this project I marked the template on to a piece of card which was inserted into the jar as an easy solution for tracing the design. You could trace out your own designs linking with furnishings in the room or a favorite image, following this method.

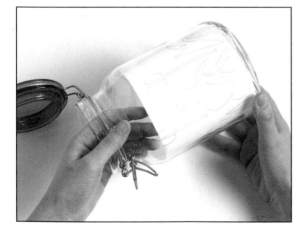

STEP 1
Trace the tulip template on to a piece of card and place inside the jar, securing it with masking tape.

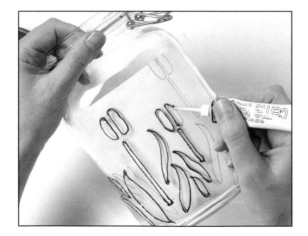

STEP 2
Use the tube of imitation lead to outline the flower design in relief.

STEP 3
Using a medium-size artist's brush, paint the blue glass paint over the background, being careful not to get any paint inside the flower or leaf shapes.

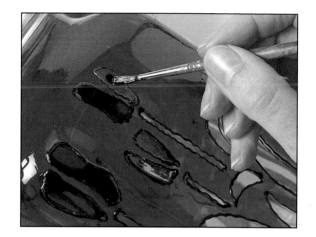

STEP 4

Paint inside the flower heads alternately in primary red and yellow.

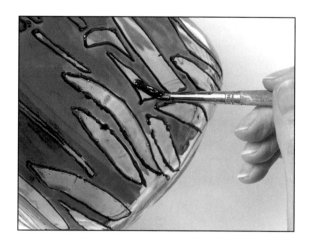

STEP 5

Finish by mixing a little yellow with blue to paint the leaves in green.

The vibrant colors of stained glass paints can be fully appreciated when they are used on items where the light will filter through the glass. Imitation lead adds definition and relief to the design.

BAY TREE DECORATIVE PANEL

THIS IS A CHARMING TECHNIQUE that can be used to transform any piece of glass, for instance a table top or a glass cabinet door, or as a decorative way to add privacy when applied to panels of glass in a door. This subtle effect is reminiscent of traditional patterned, frosted glass and is reliant upon applying a very light dusting of white spray paint.

If you want to be a bit more adventurous you can make your own *objet d'art* as I have done here, to hang as an alternative to a picture frame or a wall hanging. My local glazier cut a piece of glass ¼ inch thick with polished edges. I supplied him with the measurements and asked if he would also drill a small hole in each corner for me to use for fixing to the wall. Don't attempt to drill these holes yourself, as the glass may crack. I then cleaned the glass thoroughly with neat vinegar, before spraying the paint.

If you intend to apply this technique to a glass table top, ensure that you paint the underside, to avoid the surface being scratched or damaged when in use.

STEP 1
Cut thin strips of masking tape about ¼ inch wide and stick them down just inside the edge of the glass panel, to provide a border. Apply a light dusting of white spray paint over the entire surface and leave to dry.

STEP 2
Use the bay tree template and carefully cut out a stencil from acetate or card with a sharp craft knife.

STEP 3
Lightly spray the back of the stencil with repositional adhesive and position it carefully on to the glass panel so that the design is central.

STEP 4

Apply an even layer of white spray paint over the entire panel, ensuring that you don't miss any of the smaller leaves.

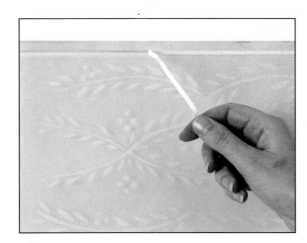

STEP 5

Immediately remove the stencil and the masking tape with care. Leave to dry completely.

It will take some patience to cut out this beautiful bay tree stencil which is made up of an intricate pattern of leaves and berries, but the spray frosting technique used here is easy to apply and quick to dry.

139

WOOD

TARNISHED BRONZE & GOLD LAMP BASE

THIS TARNISHED TECHNIQUE CAN work equally well on a variety of objects, but is particularly good when used to embellish small decorative accessories like lamp bases and picture or mirror frames. Although its rich, lustrous appearance looks difficult to achieve, it is really a question of technique and materials.

French enamel varnish is a ready-dyed shellac (like the substance used for knotting bare wood before it is painted) which has the advantage of drying very quickly and to a strong, durable, shiny finish. It can be easier to use if a little methylated spirits is added, but this will reduce the shine when it dries. It might be helpful to practice using French enamel varnish and methylated spirits in varying proportions before working on the object. However, if you do make any mistakes, respray the base gold and start again. Always spray paints in a well-ventilated room, wearing a mask. You may also wish to wear protective rubber gloves.

Before you start, ensure that the object is smooth by rubbing over with fine wire wool or fine sandpaper, then prime with one full coat of red oxide metal primer. Let the object dry overnight.

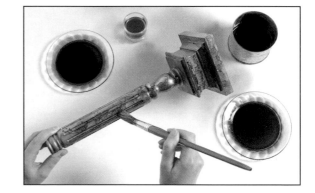

STEP 1
Cover the base evenly with gold spray, shaking the can vigorously to disperse the paint pigments inside. When using paint sprays, it is better to build the paint in thin layers letting each layer dry between coats, to avoid runs.

STEP 2
Prepare a mixture of 75% amber French enamel varnish with 25% methylated spirits. Stipple this on to the object in uneven patches, but do not cover the whole surface at this stage. Leave to dry for a few minutes.

STEP 3
Repeat Step 2, but this time cover the areas that you missed the first time, building layer upon layer. The aim at this stage is to have the object almost covered in uneven and patchy color.

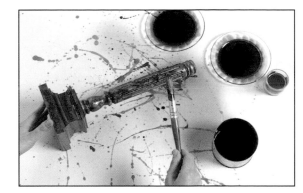

STEP 4

While the object is still wet, flick some of the undiluted brown French enamel varnish on to the surface in small amounts. These splashes will disperse the underlying layers of amber to create a wonderful natural appearance of patination. If the varnish dries too quickly, use the brush to spatter on some of the first mixture again (as in Step 2). When you are happy with the effect, leave the base to dry completely.

STEP 5

Once the object is dry, use a fine artist's brush to pick out areas of detail using black oil-based paint thinned with a little mineral spirits.

The tarnished base is complemented by a golden stenciled shade which has been created by covering it in French enamel varnish diluted in methylated spirits. The stencil was stippled in black oil-based paint.

SPATTERED GRANITE-EFFECT PLANTER

CHECKLIST

*mid-gray mat water-based
    paint*

medium-size brush

*white, black, and salmon
    pink water-based paints*

medium-size artist's brush

piece of wood or molding

polyurethane gloss varnish

THIS EFFECT IS PROBABLY one of the easiest of all paint finishes. The end result relies mainly on the combination of colors you use, and the application of technique rather than skill. This planter, which is made from medium-density fiberboard, is ideal for a polished granite effect because of its smoothness. A heavily grained wood, such as pine or oak, would not be suitable unless the grain was filled and smoothed with sandpaper.

To produce an effect reminiscent of granite, start by preparing the object with the relevant primer, then apply two coats of a mid-gray mat emulsion or equivalent water-based paint. Smooth over the surface between coats with fine sandpaper or cabinet paper. The colors you use to do the spattering should be thinned with water to a consistency of light cream. Because this effect relies on such thin mixtures of paint, it is important to spatter on to a horizontal surface, so it is advisable to finish one side of the object completely before turning over to start another. If you must work on a vertical surface, thicken the paint slightly. Before starting the project, it might pay to practice spattering on to a piece of similarly prepared card, experimenting with different size brushes (different brushes make different marks). Variations can also be created by experimenting with different colors and consistencies of paint.

It is important to give the finished item two or three coats of varnish. Not only will this protect the surface, but it will serve to enhance the polished look.

STEP 1
Once the gray base coat has dried, dip a brush into the thinned salmon pink mixture and spatter it on to the surface by hitting it sharply against a piece of wood about 8 inches from the surface.

STEP 2
Mix a darker gray color using the white and black water-based paints, and thin the mixture with water. Use this deeper color to repeat the spattering process.

STEP 3

Repeat Step 2 using first a thinned black then a thinned white mixture. Leave to dry completely.

STEP 4

Apply at least two coats of polyurethane gloss varnish to protect and enhance the surface.

The varnished subtle layers of spattered pinks and grays on this planter create a convincing polished-looking granite with real depth, which will be at home in the house or garden.

143

DECOUPAGE MAGAZINE RACK

CHECKLIST

black gloss oil-based paint

permanent spray adhesive

masking tape

fine artist's brush

gold oil-based paint

green oil-based paint

burnt umber artist's oil color

mineral spirits

cotton balls

polyurethane gloss varnish

THIS MAGAZINE RACK WAS another junk store bargain. In its original state it was only fit to be thrown away, but I felt that the shape was appealing and immediately thought of decoupage as a technique that would revitalize it as a useful and more interesting living room accessory.

Decoupage is believed to have started in Italy in the seventeenth century and quickly spread to France and England where it was widely used to beautify furniture, imitating hand-painted and inlaid work. Traditionally, an image would be glued on to an object and carefully layered with up to 40 coats of varnish which were each smoothed over between coats with the finest abrasive paper. This could have taken up to a month to complete! Fortunately, today's quick-drying varnishes let you apply many coats in a day—though six coats is usually considered sufficient.

I was inspired by these classical styles of decoupage for this magazine rack. These traditional flower cut outs were enhanced with a surrounding green and gold inlay effect and I applied many layers of gloss varnish to the finished object for a polished dramatic finish.

Before embarking on the project, apply two coats of black gloss oil-based paint, leaving it to dry overnight.

STEP 1

Cut and glue your images to the magazine rack using permanent spray adhesive.

STEP 2

Use low-tack masking tape to create a thin border to frame the central image and fill in with gold paint using a fine artist's brush. Leave to dry.

STEP 3

Using a fine artist's brush and green oil-based paint, apply thin diagonal lines across the gold paint to imitate a decorative inlay effect.

STEP 4

Enhance the shape of the object by highlighting the edges using a fine artist's brush and gold oil-based paint. Leave to dry overnight.

STEP 5

Mix a little burnt umber artist's oil color with mineral spirits and rub into the decoupaged images to antique them a little. Leave to dry and then coat the whole object with at least six layers of polyurethane gloss varnish.

Green and gold inlay has been used to surround a number of the decoupage cut outs on this completed rack. The antiqued images and highly glossed surface creates a sophisticated storage item for magazines and newspapers.

MINIATURE TORTOISESHELL CABINET

CHECKLIST

*golden yellow oil-based
    semiglosss paint*

medium-size brushes

gloss polyurethane varnish

mineral spirits

*raw sienna, burnt sienna and
    burnt umber artist's oil
    colors*

large soft brush

newspaper

fine artist's brush

masking tape

*alizarin crimson artist's oil
    color*

THIS SMALL BUT EXPENSIVE-LOOKING cabinet started life as two sets of "blank" unpainted storage boxes which I bought cheaply from a popular home furnishings store. I glued them together to make a more substantial set of drawers and made them a bit more solid looking by adding offcut moldings around the bottom and a solid pine top (this was cut from an old shelf).

For this customized cabinet I chose a paint treatment inspired by a tortoiseshell finish because I wanted to give it a deep, rich appearance, but I decided to use colors more often associated with expensive hardwoods.

When trying to achieve a sophisticated highly polished effect like this, it is important to work on a very smooth surface. It pays, therefore, to spend a bit more time on preparation. Even though these boxes were bought new and untreated, I still needed to rub down the drawers and the cabinet with medium, then fine sandpaper followed by wet and dry fine-grade abrasive paper which had been dipped in warm soapy water. I then applied three even coats of golden yellow oil-based semigloss paint, using the wet and dry paper after each coat had dried.

After finishing the project, it may take a couple of days for all the glazes to dry completely. Apply at least three even coats of high gloss varnish, smoothing down the surface between each coat with wet and dry sandpaper. Leave the final coat unsanded.

STEP 1

Thin a little gloss polyurethane varnish with mineral spirits, about half and half, and apply a thin even layer on to the dried golden yellow base coat. Working quickly, paint on diagonal patches of raw sienna, burnt sienna, and burnt umber artist's oil colors, thinned with a little mineral spirits.

STEP 2

While the colors are still wet, gently blend them together with a soft brush. Be careful not to overdo this stage; leave some of the underlying golden yellow base showing through.

STEP 3

Press a crumpled piece of newspaper on to the wet surface to create a textured effect.

STEP 4

Gently feather over the effect with a soft brush and leave to dry completely.

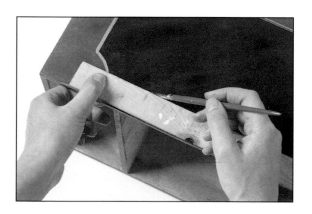

STEP 5

Mask off a paneled insert with scalloped corners. Tint some of the gloss varnish with alizarin crimson and apply it inside the panel and leave to dry. Use a fine artist's brush and a ruler to paint a gold line around the panel. Once the object is dry, protect with three coats of varnish.

New, untreated items can make excellent candidates for a paint treatment. With a little imagination, raw storage boxes have become a sophisticated miniature cabinet.

Antique Gilded Picture Frames

OLD FRAMES USUALLY END up in garbage dumps which is a pity because they are great objects to experiment on and as they come in all different shapes and sizes, it doesn't take much to transform them into individual works of art in their own right.

If you don't have any old frames lying around your home, they can easily be picked up cheaply in second-hand stores. Alternatively, you can create your own custom-made frame to fit a favorite picture. Do this by cutting offcuts of moldings or architrave with a sharp saw and a miter tool, then fix them together using wood glue, as I have done here.

Depending on the width and intricacy of the frame, almost any paint technique can be used. I chose to embellish these frames with a simple but effective imitation gilding technique which includes a final layer of tarnishing. This treatment works best on a frame which has intricate grooves, to create the most interest when the surface is burnished.

This technique does not have to be varnished and although the step that involves the fine tissue paper can be omitted, I feel it is important to include it to create a bit more texture and depth. Gold wax is available in most good artist's suppliers.

STEP 1
Apply a deep brown-red water-based paint to the whole frame and while still wet cover in fine tissue paper, pressing it into the contours of the frame. Apply another layer of the red paint and leave to dry overnight.

STEP 2
Use a soft cotton rag to apply and burnish gold wax on to the entire frame.

STEP 3

Rub gently over the contours of the frame with fine sandpaper to reveal some of the brown-red base coat underneath.

STEP 4

Flick some specks of thinned black paint sparingly over the frame using a toothbrush. As a final touch, apply in patches a mixture of polyurethane varnish tinted with burnt umber and burnt sienna and flick a small amount of mineral spirits on to the surface to disperse this mixture.

These stunning gilded frames are deceptively easy to create and will lend an air of grandeur to any room. Design your own custom-made frame from pieces of molding or architrave.

CARDBOARD

LEOPARD-PRINT FILES

CHECKLIST

*white oil-based semigloss
paint*

medium-size brushes

*raw sienna, burnt sienna and
burnt umber artist's oil
colors*

satin polyurethane varnish

small artist's brush

soft brush

THIS IS A GREAT TECHNIQUE for adding a bit of fun to those practical storage items in a home office. You can create wild and stylish patterns inspired by exotic safari wildlife on all kinds of office accessories, from cardboard file holders like these to pen holders, letter racks, and storage boxes. These designs will also appeal to children.

The golden background which I have used here for the leopard spots can also be used for tiger stripes, following the same technique. Or you can change the background to black and white and use the same method to produce zebra prints or Holstein cowhide. The beauty of these finishes is that it is the overall effect that is important, so you don't need to worry about perfecting each individual mark.

Because most of these files and boxes are made from cardboard, they don't cost much to buy, so they are ideal to practice on and if you make any mistakes or are unhappy with the results, just re-prepare them and start again. Cardboard is also ideal for instant projects, as it needs needs no preparation, other than a base coat. For this project, cover the cardboard with two coats of white oil-based semigloss paint before starting the steps.

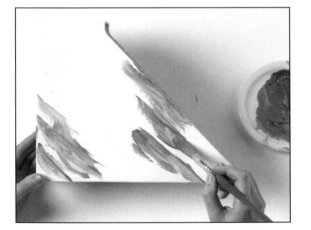

STEP 1
Mix a squeeze of raw sienna artist's oil color with a little polyurethane varnish and brush it unevenly on to the surface.

STEP 2
Use a stiff brush and flog and shuffle it through the wet glaze to create a rough stippled effect. Leave this to dry overnight.

STEP 3
Mix a squeeze of burnt sienna artist's oil color with a little polyurethane varnish and use a fine arrtist's brush to paint small incomplete circles.

To make these leopard- and tiger-print files smart enough to display, finish the insides and edges with black oil-based paint, and create a matching pen holder.

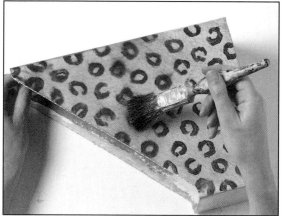

STEP 4
While the paint is still wet, gently feather a soft brush over some of the marks to soften them, but leave some of the circles looking sharp.

STEP 5
Mix a squeeze of burnt umber artist's oil color with a little polyurethane varnish and use a small brush to paint uneven edges to the marks. Leave to dry and apply at least two coats of polyurethane satin varnish.

INCANDESCENT GIFT BOXES

CHECKLIST

black spray paint

medium-size brush

blue and gold incandescent paint

toothbrush

masking tape

acetate and craft knife

metallic-gold paint

small stiff brush

EVERYONE HAS OLD AND unused boxes lying around the house. Whether they are gift, perfume, or jewelry boxes they can easily be jazzed up and recycled again as gift boxes, or as attractive containers for your own jewelry or to store small items.

The paints I have used are incandescent water-based paints which are an instant way to add a special shimmer to a gift box with minimal effort. These are available in a wide range of colors in good artist's suppliers. The resulting color of the finished box is dependent upon the base coat to which the incandescent paint is applied, so you may wish to experiment first, to see what kind of different effects can be achieved.

This idea works particularly well when a collection of these pretty containers is grouped together as an arrangement on a shelf or a table. They look equally attractive for storage in a living room, or in a bedroom. If you wish to use your boxes in a display, follow a theme linking them together as I have done here with a common color scheme. The possibilities are endless when decorating containers and as well as having fun, an enormous amount of satisfaction can be gained from giving a present in a personalized box.

Whatever the original color of your box, it is important to first create a uniform base on which to work by applying a few even coats of black spray paint.

STEP 1
Apply the incandescent blue color evenly over the box using a stippling action.

STEP 2
Continue stippling, drying the brush as you go, until the mixture disappears into the surface and you achieve a soft blue sheen.

STEP 3
Mix the gold incandescent color with a little water and flick speckles over the surface with a toothbrush. Leave to dry completely.

Create a distinctive collection of different designs for a number of lidded boxes, using stencils and masking tape to create borders, stripes, and patterns.

STEP 4

Use low-tack masking tape to mask off a border, an inner line, and a square in the middle of the box and spray with a black paint.

STEP 5

Stencil a gold flower and leaves across the center of the box using a stiff brush.

FERN-LEAF WASTEBASKET

CHECKLIST

bright green water-based paint

medium-size brush

fern leaves

spray adhesive

metallic-purple spray paint

medium-size artist's brush

orange water-based paint

acrylic varnish

THIS PLAIN WASTEBASKET has been given a bright modern design which looks dramatic but is very simple to achieve. It started out as a plain-colored functional item from an office supplier, and I planned to transform a matching set of office items including a letter holder and some ringbinder files, to sit on the desk.

Nature has always been a ready source of inspiration for artists and craftspeople, and what better way to find creative ideas from the natural world than by using things from the garden as instant templates. Experiment with other shapes such as leaves from maple or oak trees, flowers or individual petals, or strands of ivy.

Spray paints are ideal for painting anything detailed like the fronds of these fern leaves, as they are a quick way of getting paint into all the corners, leaving a crisp image behind. These types of paints are also very fast-drying, so you can complete the wastebasket easily within an hour.

Before you start the project, it is important to press the leaves or flowers first between sheets of paper in a heavy book for several days, so that they are easier to handle and will stick to the surface without curling. Give the wastebasket two layers of bright green water-based paint as a base coat, before starting the first step.

STEP 1
Lay the pressed leaves on to a covered surface and spray an even layer of adhesive on one side.

STEP 2
Place them carefully on to the wastebasket, firmly pressing down all the fronds.

STEP 3
Working in a well-ventilated area, spray metallic-purple paint in thin even layers over the wastebasket until the entire area is covered.

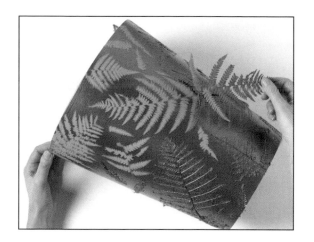

STEP 4

Let the paint dry for a few minutes, then carefully remove the leaves. You might have to use a craft knife to tease up some of the edges.

STEP 5

Using a medium-size artist's brush, paint a bright orange border around the top and bottom of the wastebasket. When the paint is dry, protect with a coat of arcylic varnish.

Leaves and flowers from the natural world create some of the most beautiful templates. Fern leaves and fronds are placed on this wastebasket at adjacent angles to produce a stunning pattern.

155

METAL

VERDIGRIS SCONCE

CHECKLIST

*gold, bronze, or copper spray
  paint*

*blue-green and mid-green
  water-based paint*

medium-size artist's brush

rag

white water-based paint

toothbrush

black water-based paint

acrylic varnish

VERDIGRIS IS THE NAME for the natural result of condensation on metals such as copper, bronze, and brass. As the metals age and are exposed to the elements, this condensation produces a beautiful bluey-green effect which has been used for green pigment in the past.

In order to create a successful verdigris effect by using a paint technique, it is best if you apply it to an object that is appropriate with the weathered effect it suggests. I found this detailed sconce at a house clearance, but you may wish to add an authentic aging effect to a modern replica, available from home improvement stores usually in an unsubtle shade of gold.

Because this finish is relatively easy to emulate, it is an ideal paint technique to experiment with. By using the same materials and paints you will achieve different results each time you try, but good results can be achieved fairly quickly. If at any stage you are not happy with the effect that is being produced, let it dry, repaint in your chosen base coat metal color (either gold, bronze, or copper) and start again.

It is important to get the right shades of blue and green paint, so if you can't find satisfactory ready-mixed colors, you may wish to either tint these paints with acrylic colors or mix your own colors from acrylics.

STEP 1
Apply a blue-green water-based paint all over the sconce, stippling the paint into the recesses.

STEP 2
Wipe the excess paint off with a soft rag to expose some of the gold base coat and leave to dry.

STEP 3
Repeat Steps 1 and 2, this time using a mid-green water-based paint and leave to dry completely.

STEP 4

Thin some white water-based paint with a little water and apply to the sconce, wiping off the excess to expose the various colors underneath. Leave to dry.

STEP 5

Use a toothbrush to flick thinned black paint spots here and there to add a bit more interest. When dry, protect the finished sconce with two coats of acrylic varnish.

An aged verdigris sconce will bring a touch of faded grandeur to any living room or dining area. Consider treating a matching candelabra with the same effect as a centerpiece for a dining table.

CRAQUELURE DELFT SCALES

CHECKLIST

red oxide metal primer spray

black and white spray paints

masking tape

medium-size artist's brushes

fine artist's brush

French ultramarine blue and alizarin crimson artist's oil colors

satin polyurethane varnish

crackle varnish

cotton balls

mineral spirits

IT WASN'T DIFFICULT TO see the potential in these old scales. A friend was throwing them away and I got quite enthusiastic about restoring them and finding a paint treatment that would enhance their appeal. They were extremely rusty, so the parts had to be dismantled and rubbed with wire wool. To get to the difficult, intricate areas I dipped a toothbrush into methylated spirits and rubbed away at the fine parts. They were then cleaned with a rag dipped in methylated spirits and left to dry before spraying them with red oxide metal primer.

I decided to use spray paints for this project because they get into intricate areas more easily and dry very quickly, letting many coats be built up in a short space of time. I sprayed the moving parts of the scales in black and the base in white and used a Delft plate as inspiration for the colors and design.. When trying to copy images like this by painting freehand lines and flowers, it is important to use good quality artist's brushes, which can make beautiful marks with just a simple stroke.

The craquelure effect was applied on top in order to enhance the images and lend an air of aged authenticity. If no hairline cracks appear an hour after you have applied the second part of the crackle varnish, heat the surface gently with a hair dryer for a few minutes. If this still produces no results, let the whole object dry overnight and repeat the process the next day, but with less drying time between the two stages.

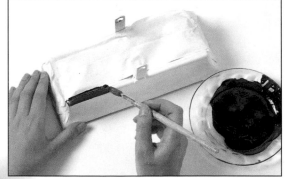

STEP 1
Mask a border around the top and bottom of the base. Paint a line around the top and bottom of the scales using a fine artist's brush and French ultramarine blue mixed with a tiny amount of alizarin crimson and a little polyurethane varnish.

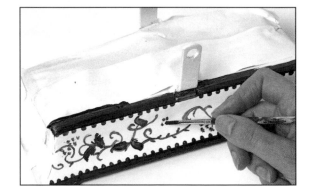

STEP 2
Paint the Delft-style pattern on the sides and top. Leave to dry overnight, then remove the masking tape and apply the first layer of the crackle varnish. Leave for about an hour until it becomes slightly tacky but not sticky, then apply the second part of the varnish and wait for cracks to appear.

STEP 3

Apply more of the blue and crimson mixture and cover the base with this, rubbing it into the cracks with cotton balls.

STEP 4

Keep wiping the excess away with cotton balls until the mixture is left to highlight the cracks. Leave to dry completely.

STEP 5

As a finishing touch, apply a protective coat of satin polyurethane varnish.

The design on these blue and white scales was inspired by the simplicity of Dutch Delft pottery. The tiny lines created by the craquelure finish are reminiscent of the hairline cracks found in the glazed surface of antique pottery.

ANTIQUE BRONZED CURTAIN ROD

CHECKLIST

medium-size artist's brushes

brown and amber French enamel varnish

methylated spirits

piece of wood or molding

DECORATIVE IRONWORK HAS SEEN something of a revival in recent years. Coat stands, wine racks, and curtain rods like this can now be bought from most department stores or good home improvement centers and are relatively inexpensive. At one time you would have had to specially commission objects like this to your own design from a local blacksmith or ironmonger.

Wrought ironwork is quite versatile and will fit in well with traditional and contemporary settings, but unfortunately such items are usually finished in mat black or dull gold like this curtain rod. I bought this one because I liked the fleur-de-lis ends but decided to enliven it a little with a paint technique that might look

difficult at first glance, but is actually very easy to achieve. French enamel varnish is shellac-based and dries very quickly, so you have to be prepared to work fast on this project. If you have trouble getting hold of French enamel varnish, you can replace it with burnt sienna and burnt umber artist's oil colors mixed with a little polyurethane varnish and spattered with white spirit instead of methylated spirits. If you have a black curtain rod, start by spraying it with an even layer of metallic-gold spray before going on to the first step.

This easy bronzing will add a touch of distinctiveness to a simple curtain rod, and could be applied to wrought-iron candlesticks or an umbrella stand in the same room.

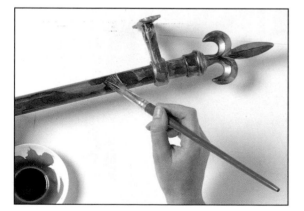

STEP 1
Apply the amber French enamel varnish in patches using a medium-size artist's brush.

STEP 2
Immediately stipple the brown French enamel varnish on to the areas of the rod which you missed in Step 1.

STEP 3
While these layers are still wet, spatter on some more of the amber color followed by methylated spirits by tapping a loaded brush against a piece of wood just above the object. Immediately repeat the process but using the brown enamel varnish.

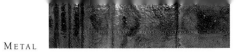

DECOUPAGE FLOWER BUCKET

THIS CHEAP BUCKET WAS bought new as unpainted tinware, which provides an ideal base for a painted project. Other basic-style tinware can be found in discount stores, such as watering cans and garden pots. The paint treatment which I chose for the bucket is based on traditional French eighteenth-century designs with its classical-style fruit and gold coach lines, which would have been applied to various decorative items.

For professional results with decoupage, it pays to take a little time to cut around your shapes carefully with very sharp scissors, keeping a craft knife on hand for any very intricate areas of detail. Traditionally, numerous coats of varnish would be applied once the object was finished. These layers serve to eliminate the relief created by the paper images, the end result being a polished, smooth surface. Depending on how thin your cut outs are, three or four coats of varnish should be sufficient.

Although decoupage is particularly good for embellishing small objects like frames or boxes, it can also be applied with a little more imagination on to larger pieces of furniture and even on walls to create interest. It can also be fun to play with scale, sticking large imagery on to small objects and vice versa.

Before starting to paint on the bucket, first prime the surface with a metal primer and leave this to dry.

STEP 1
Apply two coats of dark green water-based mat paint to the bucket. While this is drying, cut out your images with sharp scissors.

STEP 2
Spray the images with permanent adhesive and place around the bucket.

STEP 3
Using a fine artist's brush and gold paint thinned with a little mineral spirits, paint a wavy line near the top and bottom of the bucket.

STEP 4

Continue with the gold paint, applying some leaf-like shapes around the wavy line and leave to dry completely.

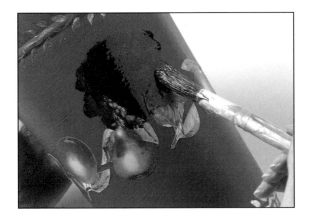

STEP 5

Mix a little burnt umber artist's oil color into some satin polyurethane varnish and apply an even coat over the whole object. Apply at least four coats of clear satin polyurethane varnish.

Plain tinware can be transformed from an item only fit to be seen in the garden or solarium, to a classical accessory for the living room, thanks to a traditional decoupage design.

POST-MODERN INDUSTRIAL BREADBIN

CHECKLIST

long-pile radiator roller

metallic-silver paint

soft pencil

wood glue

black water-based paint

medium-size brush

4 inch stiff brush

fine steel wool

satin acrylic varnish

I DECIDED TO TRY to refurbish this shabby 1950s metal breadbin more for the challenge, as well as a bit of fun. Because it was in such a state it required a radical approach and something with a bit of texture. I used a metallic-silver paint for its durability and also for the slightly rippled texture of the finish which results when it is applied with a long-pile roller. It is also a good base coat when trying to achieve a buffed and aged cast-iron effect, which is appropriate for an object of this nature.

The imitation rivets lend a bit more interest and authenticity to what would otherwise have been a very plain surface. These have been cleverly produced with small drops of wood glue, applied with a steady hand. Ensure that you mark out the position of each one with a pencil first, to avoid any misplaced blobs. This industrial finish is perfect for the modern hi-tech kitchen, and would also work well on metal garden chairs and tables, as long as they were protected from the elements with two coats of exterior varnish.

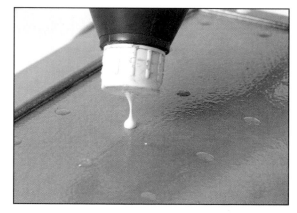

STEP 1
Apply a layer of metallic-silver paint with a long-pile radiator roller and aim to achieve an overall rippled effect. Leave to dry completely.

STEP 2
Mark out with a soft pencil the position for the imitation rivets and carefully squeeze a small drop of wood glue on to each spot. Again, leave to dry.

STEP 3
Thin some water-based black paint with about 20% water and brush over the whole object, then wipe the excess off with a rag.

STEP 4

While the paint is still wet, rub a stiff dry brush vigorously across the surface to create a distressed effect, cleaning and drying the brush on a rag when it becomes wet. Leave to dry.

STEP 5

When the surface is completely dry, use a piece of fine steel wool to burnish the surface, then apply a clear coat of satin acrylic varnish.

From a rusting and grubby item only fit for the dump, this breadbin has been revived with a stylish hi-tech finish complete with textured surface and imitation rivets, and would not look out of place in any modern kitchen.

CERAMICS & PLASTER

STARFISH PLATE

CHECKLIST

yellow, blue, and red ceramic paints

natural sponge

medium and fine artist's brushes

THIS PROJECT IS A GOOD example of how the simplest treatment can create dramatic results. What was an ordinary and uninspiring ceramic plate has been transformed into a bright and cheerful decorative accessory which can be used ornamentally or as a useful fruit dish. The secret of the striking design lies in using a good quality artist's brush to paint the starfish shapes in bold colors. The size of the brush you use will determine the size of the shapes and if you don't feel confident enough to work straight on to the plate, practice first on a piece of card or paper. However, you should always bear in mind when working on a project that requires freehand painting, that it is the imprecise lines and shapes that provide its charm; you do not want the design to look too "perfect."

Because I wanted the plate to be functional, I used ceramic paints which are baked in the oven. These paints are available in good artist's suppliers and craft stores and help to make the design much more durable. You can use solvent or cold water ceramic paints if your object is for purely decorative use.

STEP 1
Sponge on a textured background in primary yellow using a natural sponge and leave to dry.

STEP 2
Use a good quality medium-size artist's brush to paint on primary blue starfish shapes, leaving regular gaps between each shape.

STEP 3
Use a finer artist's brush to paint small asterisk shapes between the starfishes in a primary red.

Swirling freeform starfish shapes overlap the edges of this sponged plate to create a sense of movement and frivolity. Don't hide the design, but display the dish on a kitchen wall or on the shelf of a dresser.

STEP 4
Highlight the edges of some of the starfish shapes in yellow to create a three-dimensional effect.

TILED WALL PANEL

CHECKLIST

spray adhesive

acetate and craft knife

*blue, white, green, and red
   spray paints*

masking tape

fine artist's brush

blue ceramic paint

THE MAIN PROBLEM WITH applying any paint technique to a ceramic surface is long-term durability. The very reason that ceramic products are used in areas of high wear and tear such as kitchens and bathrooms, is because ceramic is easy to clean and will maintain its looks. This makes it hard to get any substance to adhere to it—including paint—as you cannot key the surface as this will scratch it. However, there are occasions when you might want to create more interest in a large area or spice up something smaller as I have done to this ceramic tiled panel. Ensure that whatever image you apply, in whatever paint medium, will not be subjected to heavy wear or need to be wiped excessively.

Because of this durability problem, I decided to make this tiled panel to hang as a purely decorative item. It was put together simply by grouting nine plain white tiles within a wooden frame made from pieces of wood recycled from my workshop. The stenciled cyclamens were created using spray paints, because of their ability to adhere to difficult surfaces.

Before starting to apply the paint, clean the ceramic surface thoroughly with a slightly abrasive kitchen scourer dipped in warm soapy water and leave to dry. Any stubborn stains can be removed with a little methylated spirits and fine steel wool.

STEP 1
Spray the classical urn template with repositional adhesive and place it on top of the lower half of the tiles.

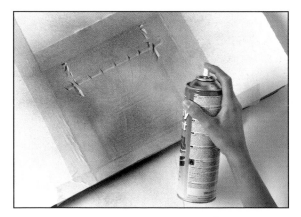

STEP 2
Mask off the surrounding area and spray a light film of deep blue paint over the image, followed by a misty layer of white spray paint. Remove the stencil and leave to dry.

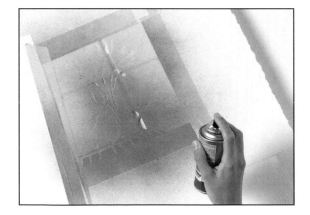

STEP 3
Place the cyclamen stencil carefully so that the base of the design sits on top of the urn. Mask off the surrounding area and spray a leaf green color over the image.

STEP 4

Spray the flowers lightly with a red paint, ensuring that the stems are protected. Carefully remove the stencil and let dry for a few hours.

STEP 5

Use a fine artist's brush and blue ceramic paint to create a border of leaves around the image.

This customized picture frame was given the final touch by finishing the wooden frame in dark blue water-based paint, followed by a crackle medium with a layer of white water-based paint on top.

TARTAN CANDY JAR

STORAGE JARS OF ANY kind are indispensable whether for the kitchen, bathroom, or bedroom. However, it is not always easy to get just what you want in the right colors. The simple remedy is to buy plain-colored ceramic jars and customize them yourself with the help of some ceramic paints.

For this small, lidded jar I decided on a simple design with bright colors as it would be used to keep candy in for the children. It is an ideal project for beginners because of its simplicity and the fact that it relies on very easy technique and readily available household materials. It shows the versatility of using masking tape for creating easy and professional-looking lines, to produce an instant tartan pattern. It is important to use a synthetic household sponge to create the very fine texture of color over the surface.

The ceramic paints I used for this project can be fired in a hot oven to bake the paints and make them more durable, or alternatively you can use solvent or cold water ceramic paints which are easier to use, though not as durable. These paints can be bought in artist's suppliers and craft stores.

STEP 1
Apply narrow-width, low-tack masking tape evenly around the jar to create vertical stripes.

STEP 2
Sponge on a bright yellow ceramic paint in uneven patterns to create a bit of texture. Remove the masking tape and leave to dry.

STEP 3
Create horizontal stripes of the same thickness using the masking tape and sponge on a lime green ceramic paint.

STEP 4

Use more masking tape to create horizontal and vertical thin blue stripes between the green and yellow stripes.

STEP 5

Stencil the candy shapes randomly around the jar in bright orange.

STEP 6

Sponge a border of yellow and lime green around the edge of the lid.

A fun finish can be created with the help of some masking tape and a household sponge. This designer tartan jar comes complete with stenciled candies, revealing its contents.

Marbled Niche

CHECKLIST

*white, black, and green
    oil-based paints*

mineral spirits

medium-size artist's brush

paper towel

natural sponge

large soft brush

feather

gold oil-based paint

fine artist's brush

gloss polyurethane varnish

This plaster cast niche was bought from a home improvement center and because plaster objects like this come unprepared, they are usually quite inexpensive.

Plaster in its unprimed state is an extremely absorbent material and it is impossible to apply almost any paint technique successfully until it is sealed and primed (sponging might be an exception). Do this by mixing a solution of wood glue with an equal amount of water and working quickly, brush an even layer all over the object taking care to avoid brushmarks and runs. If the object is quite ornate and has intricate moldings, stipple the mixture into the detailing using a smaller brush. Once this has dried, apply two coats of a white oil-based paint as a base coat.

I chose a marble finish for this decorative niche simply because it is the kind of object that might traditionally have been carved in marble and would look quite authentic and convincing in such a treatment. Marbling is one of the more difficult techniques, so it would be beneficial to practice a couple of times on a piece of card before tackling the project itself, especially when working on objects like this niche with its curves and intricate details.

Most marbling techniques like this benefit enormously from being properly varnished. This not only helps protect the object, but enhances the paint treatment and produces a more convincing look of polished marble.

STEP 1
Apply patches of black oil-based paint mixed with 50% mineral spirits, then patches of dark green oil-based paint mixed with 50% mineral spirits.

STEP 2
Dab the wet glazes with paper towel to create a mottled, uneven, ragged effect.

STEP 3
While the surface is still wet, gently dab areas with a damp sponge which has been dipped in mineral spirits. This will disperse the glaze in patches.

STEP 4

Create veins in the glaze by dragging a feather dipped in the black glaze across the surface using diagonal strokes.

STEP 5

Lightly soften the veins by feathering over with a soft brush, then leave to dry overnight.

STEP 6

Highlight selected areas of detail with a fine artist's brush and gold paint. Leave to dry, then apply at least two coats of gloss polyurethane varnish.

Link other architectural features in the room to the finished niche by giving cornicing, architrave, and baseboards the same green, black, and gold marbled treatment.

ANTIQUED AZTEC URN

CHECKLIST

soft pencil

*fine and medium-size artist's
brushes*

*cream, blue, yellow, and red
water-based paints*

burnt umber artist's oil color

polyurethane varnish

medium-size brush

THE GREAT THING ABOUT this project is that you don't have to hunt far for your source material. Terra-cotta pots come in all shapes and sizes and plain planting pots are cheap to buy in garden centers.

The patterns and colors I have used on these pots were inspired by South American tribal and ethnic art. This is a great technique for building your confidence with freehand painting with fine brushes, because the beauty and charm of the design relies on simple handpainted lines, imprecise shapes, and bright colors, all of which add to its authenticity.

Applying paint on to terra-cotta is normally problematic due to the porous nature of this type of earthenware. However, this technique works with this characteristic, using it to create a faded-looking painted pot. When working with an unsealed terra-cotta surface like this, it is helpful if you thin the paints with about 30% water; this makes them flow better and helps them sink into the terra-cotta.

When the pot is finished, the tinted varnish will produce an additional aging effect, and the pot can be used outside where weathering will add to its charm.

STEP 1
Start by lightly marking out your design around the pot with a fine soft pencil.

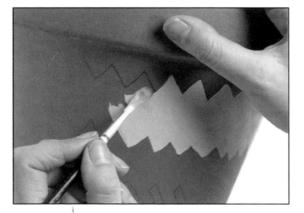

STEP 2
Paint the larger spaces in a cream water-based paint using a medium-size artist's brush.

STEP 3
Paint a detailed border around the bottom and top of the pot using a fine brush and a primary blue water-based paint.

STEP 4

Paint the smaller areas of detail using primary colors and a fine artist's brush. When you have enough detail on the pot, let it dry completely.

STEP 5

Mix a squeeze of burnt umber artist's oil color with some polyurethane varnish and paint it over the entire surface.

Ethnic designs are often based on simple repeating patterns which are easy to paint freehand, using a good artist's brush. Using thinned paints and a tinted varnish are shortcuts to help create an aged look to the finished pot.

Weathered Sundial

CHECKLIST

raw linseed oil

mineral spirits

medium-size brushes

dark green water-based paint

synthetic sponge

lime green water-based paint

fine artist's brush

gray water-based paint

coarse steel wool

No GARDEN IS COMPLETE without a range of attractive garden furniture and ornaments. Authentically aged stone statues, birdbaths, and plinths have a quality which is sadly missing from their newer counterparts, but these naturally aged items can only occasionally be found, and usually at a price.

The obvious answer is to buy a new piece of stonework from a garden center and use the magic of paint to create the "patina of age." New stonework is too white to blend in naturally in the garden, so this technique will help your plinth to age gracefully. This is created by not only adding the "graying" effect of the weather to stonework, but also by adding a bit more color in the form of dark and light greens to mimic the natural effects of moss and lichen. The linseed oil is used purely as a base color to add some initial warmth to the cold white stone. The final effect is that the finished stonework of this plinth now blends naturally as a base for an old verdigris sundial.

No initial preparation was needed to seal the stonework, as each coat of paint is meant to sink into the surface for a more natural effect.

STEP 1
Mix some raw linseed oil with a little mineral spirits and apply a generous amount liberally and unevenly over the entire base. Leave to dry.

STEP 2
Apply a dark green water-based paint in rough patches with a sponge.

STEP 3
Lightly brush over the surface with a fine artist's brush and a lime green water-based color to highlight the details. Leave to dry.

STEP 4

Mix a dirty gray wash from 50% gray paint and 50% water and apply over the entire surface. Wipe off any excess with a rag and leave to dry.

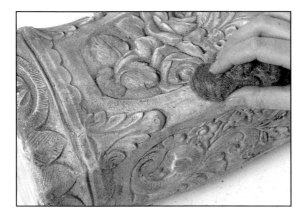

STEP 5

Wipe the surface over with coarse steel wool to expose the texture of the stonework, leaving the glazes collected in the recesses.

New stonework doesn't always weather gracefully, which means that it can turn out looking gray. However, clever use of subtle grays and greens will ensure that your painted stonework always has an attractive aged appearance.

AGED GARDEN POT

CHECKLIST

brown, moss green, and light green water-based paints

natural sponge

gold paint

fine artist's brush

off-white water-based paint

medium-size brush

mat acrylic varnish

ONE OF THE PERENNIAL problems with buying new garden ornaments and accessories is that they often look too new for too long, especially when placed alongside a rustic and mellowed patio or shed.

Instead of waiting patiently for your terra-cotta ornaments to weather and age naturally, you can hurry the process along with a few easy steps and basic materials. This cheap and simple technique will not only help your pots and urns blend in better with the garden, but can also serve to create a feature of them if arranged on a patio or in a solarium.

This effect relies upon using water-based paints thinned down to a consistency of light cream and upon taking advantage of the thirsty nature of an untreated material like terra-cotta. This lets you create a reasonably durable finish, simply because most of the thinned paint sinks into the pot. You need not worry about making "mistakes," as an uneven mottled finish is what you will be trying to achieve.

Despite the durability of this finish, it is still advisable to apply a few coats of exterior clear mat varnish for extra protection against the elements.

STEP 1
Use a natural sponge and a dark brown water-based paint thinned slightly with water, to create a patchy, textured effect.

STEP 2
Go over the pot again, sponging on an earthy moss green color, ensuring that you do not create an even effect.

STEP 3

Sponge small areas of a light green color in patches around the pot and leave to dry.

STEP 4

Pick out any details on the pot using a fine artist's brush and gold paint. Leave to dry.

STEP 5

Apply a layer of off-white water-based paint thinned with 50% water. Wipe off any excess off with a rag to give the pot an overall milky, dusty look. Leave to dry completely and apply two coats of mat acrylic varnish.

The aged patina of these painted pots relies upon careful sponging together with a final milky coat of paint to soften the effects of the greens and browns. Choose a pot with some interesting detailing around the rim, which can be highlighted in gold.

TEMPLATES

THESE TEMPLATES CAN BE used to complete each of the named projects in Part 2. To use the templates, reduce or enlarge them using a photocopier, adjusting the size according to what you are working on. For some projects, more than one template has been used.

CARNATION & TULIP TABLECLOTH
(pages 122–3)

CARNATION & TULIP TABLECLOTH
(pages 122–3)

CANVAS FLOOR CLOTH
(*pages 126–7*)

CANVAS FLOOR CLOTH
(pages 126–7)

CANVAS FLOOR CLOTH
(pages 126–7)

TILED WALL PANEL
(pages 168–9)

MISTY CLOUDS WINDOW SHADE
(pages 130–31)

CHERUB LAMPSHADE
(pages 128–9)

MISTY CLOUDS WINDOW SHADE
(pages 130–31)

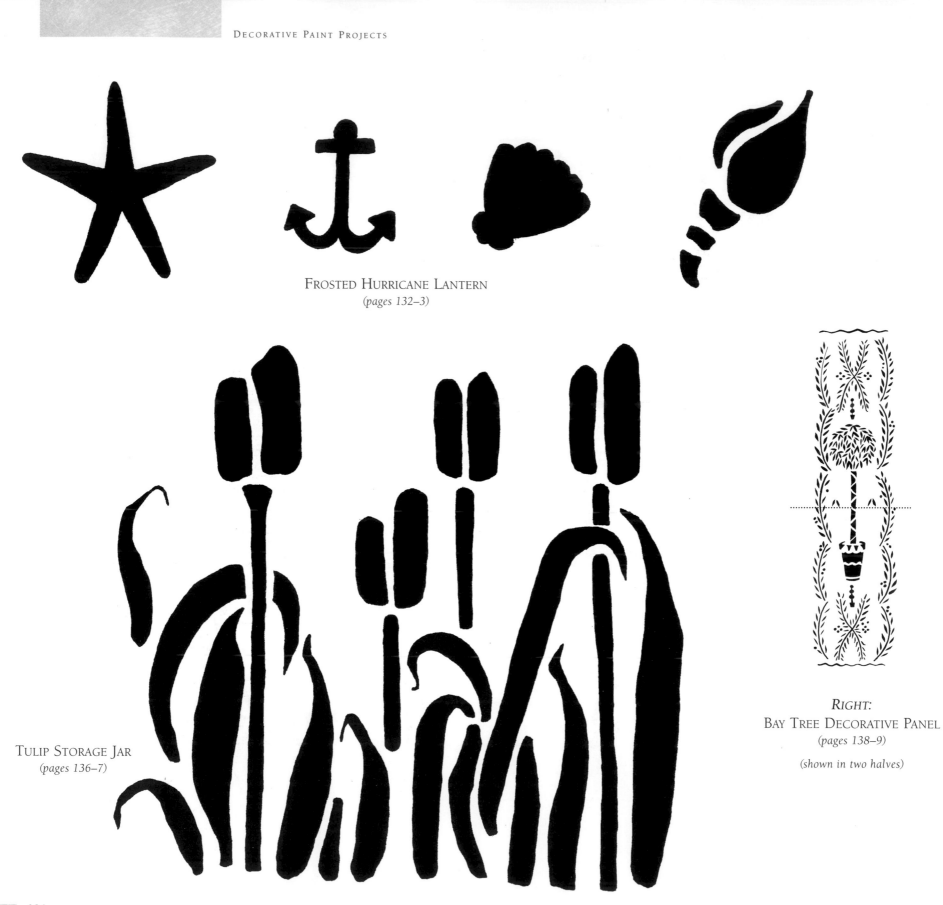

FROSTED HURRICANE LANTERN
(pages 132–3)

TULIP STORAGE JAR
(pages 136–7)

RIGHT:
BAY TREE DECORATIVE PANEL
(pages 138–9)

(shown in two halves)

TILED WALL PANEL
(pages 168–9)

TARNISHED BRONZE & GOLD LAMP BASE
(pages 140–41)

INCANDESCENT GIFT BOXES
(pages 152–3)

CRAQUELURE DELFT SCALES
(pages 158–9)

TARTAN CANDY JAR
(pages 170–71)